Reunions can be

Now that he knew of _____ _____ _____
he'd grabbed his baby daughter away from her.

Sara shook her head at Jake. "There's no need to apologize. I've seen you looking for Meggie all evening. I think you're having a hard time trying to share her, and that's understandable. After all, it's just been the two of you since she was born."

That she read him so well came as no surprise to Jake. Sara had always understood him. But it was disconcerting that she still did after all these years.

His eyes strayed to her lips, and he found himself wondering if they tasted the same. Feeling the need to know, his head dipped and his lips lightly brushed hers. Sara responded. Her lips clung for a second, for two, before she pulled away.

Jake wanted to kiss her again, but his eyes met hers and he saw the confusion in them. What could he possibly be thinking? Sara was not in his future. She'd opted out of his past. Hadn't he learned anything over the years?

JANET LEE BARTON has lived all over the southern U.S., but she and her husband plan to stay put in Southern Mississippi where they have made their home for the past six years. With three daughters and six grandchildren between them, they feel blessed to have at least one daughter and her family living in the same town. Janet loves being able to share her faith through her writing. Happily married to her very own hero, she is ever thankful that the Lord brought Dan into her life and wants to write stories that show that the love between a man and a woman is at its best when the relationship is built with God at the center. She's very happy that the kind of romances the Lord has called her to write can be read by and shared with women of all ages, teenagers to grandmothers alike.

Family
Circle

Janet Lee Barton

Heartsong Presents

To my Lord and Savior for showing me the way.
To my family for their love and encouragement always.
To my church family for rejoicing with me, and
To the real 'Teddy Bear Brigade' for your inspiration.
I love you all.

A note from the author:
*I love to hear from my readers! You may correspond with me
by writing:* **Janet Lee Barton**
Author Relations
PO Box 719
Uhrichsville, OH 44683

ISBN 1-58660-314-0

FAMILY CIRCLE

Cover illustration by Randy Hamblin.

PRINTED IN THE U.S.A.

one

Jake Breland pulled himself out of the nightmare, drenched with sweat and shaking all over. His heart beat so hard he could hear it. That meant he was alive, didn't it?

Slinging the tangled covers aside, he stumbled down the hall to Meggie's room. The nightlight cast a warm glow over the room, and as soon as he heard her soft, even breathing coming from the crib, he let go of the breath he'd been holding. Meggie was all right and he *was* alive. It was just the nightmare. Again. The nightmare was coming so often now, he dreaded going to bed.

Jake bent over and inhaled the sweet baby scent of his daughter. He forced himself not to pick her up and hold her. There was no sense ruining her peaceful sleep. As he watched her, his own heartbeat returned to normal. He leaned over and placed a feather-light kiss on her forehead. Meggie stirred, and afraid she'd sense his presence and wake up, Jake quietly backed out of the room. Pausing at the door to his bedroom, he shook his head and made his way down the darkened hall to the kitchen. He wouldn't be able to sleep after that dream. Besides, he had some thinking to do.

Flipping the light switch on, he looked at the clock and sighed. He might as well call it a night and put the coffee on. Leaning against the cabinet, he waited for the coffee to finish brewing and shivered as the cool night air hit his still-damp back.

He rubbed his temples and closed his eyes. All he could see was a replay of the nightmare, Meggie crying and crying and crawling all over the apartment while he lay unconscious or dead in his bed. It always ended the same—with Meggie crying out, and no one there to hear her cries. No one.

5

Jake shuddered. What if it were real? What if something did happen to him and no one was nearby to take care of Meggie?

He hadn't been able to find a suitable housekeeper since Mrs. Morrow broke her arm, so he'd had no choice but to put Meggie in daycare. He doubted the staff would check on her if she missed a day. They'd just figure he'd kept her at home. It might be days or weeks before someone would find Meggie. By then what could happen to her?

Jake shook his head, pushing the horrible images from his mind. The thought of Meggie having no one to care for her was more than he could deal with. He poured his coffee and wandered into the living room. Picking up the remote, he turned the TV on, keeping the volume low, but he stared at the screen without seeing.

When had these nightmares started? Not in the first few weeks following Melissa's death. He'd been too busy trying to accept the loss of his wife and be both mother and father to his newborn baby to sleep much at all. In the following months he'd had the dreams sporadically, but not until recently, when there'd been talk of opening an office overseas and putting him in charge, had they started coming almost nightly.

Suddenly he knew that wasn't an option. He wasn't taking Meggie halfway around the world, and he wasn't leaving her. He didn't need a partnership in a prestigious law firm. He needed more time with his daughter.

Back home, he wouldn't have to set up his own practice. His cousin John had asked him to come into partnership with him more than once. With two of them to share the workload, there'd be more time for Meggie.

Jake sighed and ran his fingers through his tousled hair. He'd never planned or wanted to move back home. Now he had his daughter to think of. He couldn't put it off any longer.

He might not have family here in Albuquerque to make sure Meggie was all right, but he had them in southern New Mexico, in his small hometown of Sweet Springs. Family who'd offered over and over to help. He had to make sure that if anything happened to him, she'd have someone right there, right away. It was time. Time to go home.

⁂

Sara Tanner tied off the embroidery thread and looked at her work with a critical eye. She held it up for her grandfather's inspection. "How's it look, Grandpa? If you were two or three, would it appeal to you?"

William Oliver lowered the newspaper he'd been reading, looked over the top of his bifocals, and chuckled. "It appeals to me at seventy, Darlin'. I'm sure it would appeal to me if I were a child." He got up from the kitchen table and brought the coffeepot over to refill their cups.

"They are cute, aren't they? I'm so glad we decided to do this." Sara slipped the finished teddy bear into a bag with the others she'd made that week.

"You ladies at church do some real good things. I bet those little bears will mean a lot to the small children brought into the emergency room."

Sara took a sip of coffee and nodded. "That's what we're hoping. The hospital thought it was a great idea. We'll know for sure soon. I'm going to pick up the rest and deliver them tomorrow afternoon."

"Tomorrow?" Her grandfather slapped his forehead. "I forgot to tell you—Nora called. You've been summoned to lunch tomorrow."

Sara sighed and shook her head. "That's an apt description of her invitations, if I ever heard one. I dread going. She's just going to try to convince me to move out to the ranch again."

"That's the last place you need to be."

"I know, Grandpa, and I've told her it's not going to happen. I'm running out of ways to say no, but she was Wade's mother. I can't just tell her to get lost."

Her grandfather grinned and nodded. "Even though that's exactly what you should do."

Sara chuckled. "No, I shouldn't, but I have to admit I'd

certainly like to at times."

"Well, Darlin', I don't like the way she wants to control your life. You've had enough of that."

Sara reached across the table to squeeze his hand. "I'm not going to let her control me, Grandpa. I promise." She made the promise to herself, too. Her mother-in-law could be over-powering at times. She changed the subject. "What are you going to do tomorrow?"

"I'm not sure. I have my garden planted. Ben and Lydia are away at a livestock auction, so we won't be having our regular chess game. Got plenty of time on my hands. Want me to go with you to Nora's?"

Sara chuckled. Bless his heart. "That's a great idea, Grandpa. Do you think you can put up with her for that long?"

"Nora's no problem for me. I'll be fine. Besides, that cook of hers is worth it."

Sara laughed, circling the table to hug him. "I don't know what I'd do without you."

He hugged her back. "Nope, it's the other way around, Sara. I was just rambling around this old house 'til you moved in. You take real good care of me."

Tears pooled in Sara's eyes. They were a pair, the two of them. She knew who'd been taking care of whom. Until a few months ago, she'd been the one on the receiving end of all the care from her grandfather, her husband's family, and her church family. "Thank you, Grandpa. I love you."

"Guess I'll be calling it a night," he said after clearing his throat. "I love you, Honey. I'm proud of the way you're getting on with things." He nodded his head and pushed away from the table. "Real proud. Just don't let Nora tell you how to live your life."

"I won't. You sleep well." She gave him another hug and took their cups to the sink.

It took only a few minutes to clean up the kitchen. Not yet ready for bed, Sara slipped out to sit in the front-porch swing.

Putting it in motion, she caught the delicate smell of the lilac bush behind her.

It felt so good to notice small things again: the sweet smell of the honeysuckle climbing the trellis, the soft feel of the gentle breeze. How bright the stars shone down. Spring was here. Everything was coming to life, and for the first time in a long time, Sara felt alive.

Bowing her head, she said a silent prayer of thanksgiving for Grandpa, all of the Tanners and Brelands, and her church family. It'd taken them all to get her through the past year. She wouldn't have made it without them. Most of all, she thanked the Lord for seeing to it that she'd had them to help her.

She couldn't wait until fall, when she'd be returning to her teaching job at the high school. She'd just have to keep herself busy until then—and convince Nora that she was not moving to the ranch. Period. Easier said than done. Her mother-in-law did not like to take no for an answer. Sara could just picture the two of them living together. Two widows growing old together. The thought drew a shudder from her. Maybe she would cancel tomorrow's lunch with Nora, after all. There would be other lunches. There always were.

Sara kept the swing in motion until her eyes grew heavy. She hadn't had trouble sleeping for several months, but still, she didn't like to go to bed until she was almost asleep on her feet. Entering the house quietly, she locked the door and went upstairs. She'd sleep well tonight. She was sure of it.

☙

Sara felt she'd taken the coward's way out by canceling her lunch with Nora, but her excuse of having to pick up those adorable teddy bears was a valid one. Besides, she didn't want lunch with Nora to put a damper on her good mood.

One more stop and she'd have the last of the teddy bears gathered up. She was excited about taking them to the hospital. All of the ladies had been so eager to help make them, and the hospital was thrilled with the offer. If having a teddy bear to cuddle while receiving medical attention could ease the fear of just one child, their work would be well worth the hours spent.

She pulled to a stop at the curb in front of Ellie Tanner's house and hurried down the walk and up the porch steps. "Gram?" Sara called, opening the screen door. "You here?"

"Back here, Sara. In the kitchen," came the reply.

Bypassing the living room, Sara hurried through the dining room into the sunny kitchen at the back of the house. The sight of Gram sitting at the table watching an adorable baby girl attempt to feed herself stopped Sara in her tracks. Her heart twisted and turned, and she forgot to breathe until Gram turned in her seat and said, "Sara?"

Sara forced the air out of her lungs and tried to smile.

Gram quickly got up and led her to a chair. "Oh, my dear Sara. I'm so sorry. I didn't even think to warn you."

Sara blinked quickly to hide the tears that threatened and shook her head. "No, Gram. It's fine. I. . .I just didn't expect to see a baby at your table." She forced her gaze off the child.

Sara patted the older woman's hand that still rested on her shoulder. "I'm fine, Gram. Really. But who is this little beauty? Who are you doing a favor for now?"

Gram gave Sara a warm hug and took her seat once more, handing the baby another chicken stick and being rewarded with a huge grin.

"This is my great-granddaughter Meggie, Jake's daughter. This is Sara, Meggie." She turned back to face Sara. "He finally came to his senses and decided to move back home. He's going to join John's firm as a partner." Gram handed the baby a cup of milk as she continued her explanation. "They're discussing it all over lunch."

Jake. Back here. Sara's heart seemed to screech to a stop before it jumped into high gear. Her gaze snapped back to the baby. *Jake's baby.* The little girl had his dark hair, his eyes, and his coloring. Meggie grinned at her, and Sara saw a miniature dimple—exactly like the one Jake had. Like the one she used to tease him about, just so he'd grin at her. She'd stand on tiptoe and plant a quick kiss on the dimple before it disappeared. She shook her head to clear the vision she'd conjured in her mind.

Sara wasn't sure she was ready to see her first love after all these years and all that had happened. She started to her feet just as Gram set a cup of tea in front of her. When had Gram made it? How long had she been sitting there staring at the baby?

She tried to sound calm. "I just came by to pick up the teddy bears, Gram. I really need to get to the hospital."

"After you drink that tea, Child. You aren't driving anywhere right now. Not until I know you're all right."

Realizing she was not in any shape to drive, Sara nodded her head and took a sip of the hot, sweet liquid. *Lord, please get me through this. You've helped me with everything else, please help me over this new hurdle.*

"Sara."

Sara pulled her gaze from the baby, who shyly glanced from Gram to Sara and back again.

"Yes, Ma'am?"

"Is it seeing a baby or the fact that Jake is moving back that's upsetting you?"

Gram always did have a way of zeroing in on a problem. Sara was saved from answering when the baby suddenly let out a wail and banged the tray, sending her food flying and milk splashing. The wail quickly turned to giggles, and the baby started bouncing up and down in her seat.

Sara couldn't help but laugh. Milk was dripping off the tray and running down the baby's face, and Gram's lap held an assortment of finger food.

"Why, you little minx!" Gram laughed and looked around as if unsure what to do next.

"I'll clean up the mess, Gram. It won't take a minute."

Sara grabbed the washcloth the older woman had handy and started to wipe off the baby's face while Gram emptied her lap, still chuckling.

Sara's heart turned over as Meggie reached out and clung

to her blouse, trying to climb out of the high chair. The baby's grip tightened as Gram tried to take her.

In that moment, Sara's heart melted. "It's okay. I'll take her."

Gram chuckled. "I don't think she's giving you much choice. This one has a mind of her own." She took the cloth from Sara to finish cleaning up the mess.

Sara managed to unhook the safety belt keeping the baby in place, and Meggie lunged, climbing into Sara's arms. The baby held on for dear life and hid her face in the curve of Sara's neck. Sara's arms tightened around Meggie, and she murmured soothing noises to the baby, finding that the one thing she'd been avoiding for months was exactly what she needed. The feel of a baby in her arms. Closing her eyes, she cuddled Meggie close and sighed deeply. *Lord, thank You. You always seem to know what I need, when I need it.*

Finished with the cleanup, Gram turned to Sara. "I can take her now." She held her arms out to Meggie, but the baby clung to Sara.

"If you don't mind, I'll just hold her a little longer."

"You're sure?" Gram asked, concern etching her face.

Sara nodded and took her seat again. "I'm sure. I think this is just what we both need."

Gram looked closely at the two and nodded. "I think you may be right." She freshened up their tea and peeked at Meggie. "Her eyes are closed. I wonder if she's asleep or just playing possum."

Sara gently tightened her hold on the baby. "Doesn't matter to me. I'll just enjoy holding her close as long as she'll let me."

Gram nodded and tears gathered in her eyes. "Sara, you will have another one of your own, one day. The Lord will see to that."

Sara rubbed Meggie's back lightly, enjoying the feel of the warm little body in her arms. "I hope so, Gram. He brought me here today, and He knew how badly I needed the feel of a baby in my arms, even before I did." She closed her eyes and inhaled the sweet, powder scent of Meggie.

"I guess we all thought it would be too painful for you. Maybe we've been a bit overprotective."

"No, Gram. You've all been wonderful. I don't know what I would have done without you."

"I'm just glad Jake has realized he can use some help."

Not wanting to be rude, Sara forced herself to respond to the change of subject. "Will he be staying with you or at the ranch with Luke?"

"He's going to stay here with me." Gram's smile showed her pleasure at having her grandson back in town. "He says he wants to find a house in town or build one, since his office will be here. He doesn't want to commute back and forth from the ranch."

Although unsure of how she felt about seeing Jake again, Sara still felt curious about his reasons for coming back. He'd said once that he couldn't wait to get out of Sweet Springs. "What made him decide to move back? Did he say?"

"Just that Meggie needed to know her family, and he knows someone will be here for her if something should happen to him." Gram sighed. "He's not the same Jake. He seems bitter, angry."

"That's not so unusual, Gram. I had to get over a lot of that, too."

"But that's just it, Sara. You have gotten on with your life. You are dealing with it. Jake hasn't."

"I had all of you to help me."

Gram nodded her head. "And you let the Lord heal you. I don't think Jake is on speaking terms with Him. And without that, I'm not sure how much help the rest of us can be to him."

Sara pushed thoughts of how much Jake had hurt her to the back of her mind. That was the past and had nothing to do with the present. She could relate to the pain he was going through now and felt only sorrow that he might be at odds with the Lord. "We'll just have to pray. You know the Lord doesn't let go of His children."

The older woman patted Sara's hand. "I do know that, but I seemed to have forgotten for the moment. Thank you for reminding me." She reached over and brushed her fingers through the fine hair of the now gently snoring baby and smiled at Sara. "She's certainly taken up with you. You'll be all right while I gather up the teddy bears?"

Sara glanced down at the sleeping baby and smiled. "We'll be fine. I'm in no hurry to let her go."

As Gram left the room, Sara took in every detail of the sweet-smelling infant. Little hands with the tiny indentations where knuckles would one day be. She rubbed a finger over a soft, pudgy hand, and Meggie smiled in her sleep. Fine, dark hair curled softly around the cherubic face. Thick, dark eyelashes hid midnight blue eyes that Sara knew she'd inherited from Jake. She really was a beauty.

Sara's sigh was ragged. A baby with no mother. A mother with no baby. Each receiving comfort from one another. She brushed her lips gently over Meggie's velvety cheek, and try as she might, she couldn't stop the tear that escaped and slid down her face.

Hearing footsteps in the hall, Sara quickly brushed her hand across her cheek, not wanting Gram to catch her crying. She forced a smile and looked up as the footsteps came to a stop just inside the kitchen door.

The breath caught in her throat as she looked up into the eyes of Jake Breland.

ɚ

Jake returned to his grandmother's house feeling better than he had in months. He was surprised at how good it felt to be home. He was looking forward to the partnership he and his cousin John were forming. Meggie was with Gram. There would always be someone in Sweet Springs to care for her if he couldn't. A huge weight had been lifted, and he found himself whistling as he entered the house. He heard a noise coming from the kitchen and headed there. Just inside the door, he stopped in his tracks.

Jake had known this moment would come. He'd tried to prepare himself for seeing her again. But no way had he prepared himself for the sight of Sara holding his child. The woman he'd loved so long ago cradling the child of the woman who'd come between them. How could something that seemed so wrong look so right? What was she doing here, holding his daughter so close?

"Sara." His stomach did a nosedive and he clenched his fists. "Is something wrong with Meggie? Where's Gram? Is she all right?"

Jake watched the color drain from Sara's face as she quickly shook her head. "Everything is fine. Gram went upstairs to get some things I have to deliver to the hospital. That's what I stopped by for," she quickly assured him.

Jake nodded and relaxed his fingers, relieved that nothing was wrong. "I see you've met my Meggie."

Sara nodded and looked down at his sleeping daughter. "She's beautiful, Jake. I'm. . .sorry about Melissa. I should have written, called. . . ."

Jake shook his head as he crossed the room. "Don't worry about it." He knew his words sounded gruff. He couldn't help it. He wasn't sure what to say to Sara after all this time. "I'm sorry about Wade."

He watched Sara swallow and saw his pain mirrored in her eyes. She nodded. "I know." She bit her bottom lip before continuing. "I didn't know you were moving back to Sweet Springs. Gram just told me."

Jake rubbed the back of his neck, feeling more uncomfortable by the minute. "I didn't know I was moving back until a few weeks ago, and I didn't tell anyone until I got here," he said, wondering why he felt the need to explain his presence.

Seeing Sara again made him wonder if he'd made the right decision. But one glance at Meggie, and he knew he'd had no choice. It was for her sake he'd decided to come home.

Seeing more questions in Sara's eyes, questions he knew he might never be able to answer, Jake turned away to pour himself a cup of coffee. "She wasn't too much for Gram, was she?"

"No, I don't think so." Sara chuckled. "She got a little exuberant with her lunch and dumped most of it onto Gram's lap, but that was nothing."

Jake smiled, even as he noted the hint of nervousness in Sara's voice. "That's my Meggie. Mealtime is an adventure for her."

Turning back to Sara, he leaned against the cabinet. The years had been good to her. She didn't look much older than the last time he'd seen her. Auburn hair was pulled back into a clasp at the base of her neck, instead of up into a ponytail as she'd once worn it. Her deep green eyes were still as large and inviting as the creek on a hot summer day. Her smile seemed strained, yet her presence was calmer, more serene than he remembered, despite the pain in her eyes.

He looked away and cleared his throat. "I didn't give Gram much notice that I was moving back. I hope it won't be too much for her to help me out with Meggie for a little while, until I can get settled and find a housekeeper." Was Gram all he could talk about? He could remember a time when he'd had no trouble finding things to say to Sara. If there had been a lull in the conversation, he certainly hadn't stood around wondering what to say next. He'd have pulled her into his arms and kissed her. His gaze strayed to her full lips. Yes, that's what he would have done. But he couldn't do that now.

"I don't think there's much that Gram isn't willing or able to take on," Sara said, breaking into his thoughts. "She's delighted to have a baby to make over." She motioned toward the hallway. "She should be back down soon."

Jake knew she was as anxious for Gram's presence as he was. When he'd come into the kitchen to find Sara holding Meggie, it'd been obvious that she felt completely at home. Now she seemed as uncomfortable as he felt. He should know that nothing stayed the same. The easy relationship he and Sara had once shared was a thing of the past. Like it or not, he was going to have to deal with it. Just like he'd dealt with everything else. Alone.

When he glanced at Sara again, he saw that her attention was on Meggie, and the tenderness with which she looked down at his daughter was so compelling, it reached out to him. Suddenly, he felt threatened. Without knowing why, he was filled with a compulsion to hold Meggie in his arms.

He crossed the distance between them in two strides and held out his arms. "I'll take her now," he said abruptly.

Trying not to wake Meggie, Sara stood and quickly shifted the baby into Jake's arms. The flood of longing she felt in relinquishing the little girl didn't surprise her. She knew it was natural. But she was totally unprepared for the flash of awareness shooting up her arm when she brushed against Jake's arm during the transfer. Stepping back, she hoped he wouldn't notice her shaking. She wished she could just leave without the teddy bears she'd come to collect, but that would raise all kinds of questions with Gram—questions she wasn't ready to face. Sara forced herself to sit back down at the table and take a sip of her now lukewarm tea.

"I'll just put her in her crib," Jake said, his voice sounding husky. "I'll see what's holding up Gram while I'm up there." He turned and started out of the room. "Good-bye, Sara."

"Good-bye, Jake."

Only it wasn't good-bye, Sara thought as she watched him leave, his back stiff and straight. She and Jake both lived here now. Sweet Springs was a small town. There was no way they could avoid seeing each other. Obviously he was as uncomfortable around her as she was near him. Wishing things could be different didn't make them so, and she was going to have to get used to running into Jake and Meggie.

Sara took a deep breath. She could handle it. But only with the Lord's help. She knew she didn't have the strength to do it on her own.

"Sara, I'm sorry I took so long. I had to finish up one little bear's face." Gram bustled into the kitchen. She took one look at Sara and plunked down in a chair next to her. "I ran into Jake upstairs. Did he say something to upset you?"

Sara shook her head. Jake hadn't said much of anything. But neither had she. "No, Gram. I think we were both just a little uncomfortable with each other."

Gram nodded in agreement. "That's to be expected. You were both young and in love once. Then you went your separate ways."

"How did you know—"

"You young people. You think we old ones don't have eyes?" Gram chuckled. "It was obvious. The whole family thought an engagement was imminent. Then Jake went off to college and ended up marrying Melissa, and you married Wade a year later. I always wondered if you married him on the rebound," she stated bluntly.

"Gram! I loved Wade. He was a wonderful husband." Sara's insides churned. She just couldn't deal with this now, not after seeing Jake again. She had to get out of here.

"I know you loved him, Dear. And you were a wonderful wife to him, but. . .I also know you once loved Jake. . .and that he loved you." Gram reached over and patted Sara's hand. "I'm not trying to meddle. I'm just saying that the uncomfortable feelings won't last forever. You and Jake care too much about each other."

Sara stood and gathered up her purse and the bag of teddy bears, shaking her head. "I don't know. I think we've both changed too much." She bent and kissed the top of the older woman's head. "But don't you worry about it. Okay?"

"I'll walk you out." Gram rose from the chair. "You be sure and let me know how they like those little bears, you hear?"

They made their way back to the front door, and Gram gave Sara a hug. "Don't you let the fact that Jake is here keep you away, Sara. You're family too, you know."

Only by marriage. And since Wade's death, not even that. But she loved Gram and didn't want to cause her any pain by reminding her. "Thanks. I'll let you know how our bears go over." After a quick good-bye, Sara forced herself to step sedately down the walk rather than running away like she wanted to.

Starting her car, she took off and tried to shake the sudden feeling of loss that invaded her. She loved Gram and her extended family, but it wasn't going to be the same now. It couldn't be—not with Jake back in town.

❧

Jake stepped back from the hall window and started down the stairs, relieved that Sara was leaving yet feeling like a heel. He'd been rude to her. He knew that. It'd just been such a shock to see her sitting in the kitchen, completely at home, holding his child in her arms. The aura of peace surrounding them had pulled a yearning from him so strong, so unexpected that he'd felt lost, alone, on the outside looking in.

Only holding Meggie close and rocking her for a few minutes before he put her to bed had helped. He was just now beginning to realize that he needed Meggie as much as she needed him. She was the only thing in his life that made it worth living.

He entered the kitchen to find his grandmother sipping a cup of tea. He poured himself a fresh cup of coffee and joined her at the table.

"Is Meggie still sleeping?" she asked.

Jake leaned back in his chair and nodded. "I guess the trip wore her out."

"Changes do that to children, sometimes. She sure took a liking to Sara."

Knowing his grandmother, Jake sensed there was more coming. "Seemed like it. Sara certainly seems to feel at home here."

Gram looked him in the eye. "Why shouldn't she? She was married to your cousin. She's family."

Jake felt defensive. "Only by marriage."

"Jake Breland!" Gram set her cup down so hard, tea sloshed over the side. "When did that ever make a difference in this family?"

Jake knew it never had. He wouldn't have wanted it to. But the bad feelings he'd had for Wade colored his judgment and made him continue. "Well, Wade's gone now."

"Yes. He is. And if it'd been you instead of Melissa who'd died, she would still be a part of this family. Jake, I can't believe how insensitive you've become."

"You're right, Gram. I'm sorry." And he was. But he still couldn't come to terms with the past. Not after seeing Sara again.

"Well, that's something. Maybe there is still enough of the old Jake left to feel some compassion. After all, Sara has gone through as much pain as you have. More."

"How could that be?"

Gram closed her eyes and shook her head. "You lost your wife in childbirth, and I know it was devastating." When she opened her eyes, tears filled them. She reached over and covered one of his hands with hers. "I know it still is, Jake. But you have your child. Sara not only lost Wade in that car accident, she lost the baby she was carrying."

two

•

Jake's stomach clenched. Lowering his head, he willed himself to swallow past the knot in his throat and breathe normally. Sara had lost a baby. He hadn't known she was pregnant. No wonder she'd looked so bereft when he'd taken Meggie from her. Tears stung the back of his eyes, and he blinked rapidly to hold them back. Once he thought he had control, he looked at his grandmother. "Why didn't someone tell me?"

Gram ran her hand over her own teary eyes. "You were dealing with your own pain, away from us all. We didn't think you needed anything more to deal with."

Jake propped his elbows on the table and cradled his head with his hands. He thought about Meggie sleeping peacefully upstairs, and for the first time in a long time, he thanked the Lord for sparing him the pain Sara must feel.

"Did she lose it in the wreck?" Jake realized how little he knew about Wade's death. He didn't even know if Sara was with him.

"Because of it, yes." Gram got up to refill his coffee cup. When she sat back down, she clasped her hands together. "Wade was killed instantly, but Sara was put in intensive care. There were internal injuries. I know they did the best they could, but she lost the baby the next day."

She wiped her eyes with her apron. "We thought we were going to lose Sara too. Only the Lord and prayer brought her through."

Jake cleared his throat. "She seems to be dealing with it all very well." Except for when he'd taken Meggie from her.

Gram nodded. "She's come a long way, Jake. A long way. Today was the first time she's held a baby since she lost her

21

own. I didn't think to warn her Meggie was here before she came to get the teddy bears. But they took to each other right off, and she said she'd been needing to hold a baby for so long."

Jake walked over to the open back door. Leaning against the doorframe, he looked out on the backyard and shook his head. "I wish I'd known, Gram."

Maybe he'd have thought before he practically yanked Meggie away from Sara. What must she be thinking? He hadn't even mentioned being sorry about her losing the baby. He was going to have to talk to her, try to explain.

The front screen door slammed, and they heard footsteps and voices heading for the kitchen. His brother Luke and cousin John were arguing over the pros and cons of their favorite baseball teams as they reached the kitchen doorway.

"Shh." Gram put her finger to her mouth. "We have a sleeping baby upstairs and you two sound as though you're trying to be heard over the crowd at that game you're talking about."

The two men looked at each other and shrugged, tiptoeing the rest of the way into the kitchen.

"Sorry, Gram." Luke bent down and gave her a kiss and a hug. He grinned at Jake. "Hi, big brother. When's the little darlin' due to wake up? I sure would like to see her."

"So would I," John added. "We came over just to see her." He pulled two cups out of the cabinet and filled them for himself and Luke. "And to see if Gram would take pity on us bachelors and invite us to supper."

She got up from the table and thumped him on the shoulder. "When have you ever had to ask?"

John chuckled and gave Gram a kiss on the cheek, being careful not to slosh coffee on her. "It's so good to know we're always welcome at your table."

"You are. As long as you remember I just cook. You three have cleanup duty."

Luke saluted her. "Yes, Ma'am!" He kissed her other cheek.

Gram shook her head and went about getting supper started.

"You're awful quiet, Jake. Not regretting moving back already, are you?" John asked.

Jake shook his head in response to his cousin's question, although he was wondering if he'd made a major mistake. It'd been much harder than he'd realized it would be to see Sara again. And now he was going to have to see her sooner than he'd like so he could apologize for this afternoon.

"Gram just told me about Sara. About her losing the baby. I didn't know." Jake looked pointedly at his brother.

"Yeah, well, you had a lot to deal with about that time," Luke replied.

"Still, someone should have told me. I didn't even tell her I was sorry about the baby when I saw her today." Jake saw Luke and John exchange a look.

"I'm sorry, Jake. We just didn't know how to go about it," Luke said. "There was so much grief in the family around that time. Sara will understand."

Would she? Jake hoped so. But he was going to have to explain soon. He couldn't let her think he was totally unfeeling.

A cry from the second floor signaled Meggie was awake. All three men jumped to their feet. Jake was first up the stairs with Luke right behind him. John tried to overtake Luke but was pushed back.

"Hey, John, I'm the uncle," Luke protested. "You're just a cousin. You have to wait your turn."

The conversation drifted down to the kitchen where Gram was busy pulling out a skillet. She rolled her eyes and chuckled. Boys would be boys. Luke and John would be good for Jake. He needed the bantering, teasing love of his family. They'd do all they could to help him adjust to moving back. With the Lord's help, he'd heal.

🙞

Sara felt a little better as she left the hospital. At least for a short while she'd been able to push Jake to the back of her mind. The bears had been a big hit with the nurses on duty. She'd even seen how well they would go over with the children when little Ricky Monroe was brought in with a gash on his head. He'd been climbing up to his tree house when his foot slipped and he fell, scraping his head in the process. He'd been really frightened of being sewn up until the nurse handed him the little bear to hold on to. He was so busy checking it out, the stitches were finished before he knew it.

The ladies would be so pleased. She reminded herself to call Gram later, hoping Jake wouldn't answer the phone. *Jake.*

She still couldn't believe he was back in town. Gram was right; he'd changed. He seemed older than his years, aloof and lonely. He was very protective of Meggie; that was obvious. Or maybe she was misreading him. Maybe he just hadn't wanted *her* to hold his child.

Sara sighed. So much had changed. Neither of them were the same people they'd been all those years ago. She didn't know this Jake at all. Still, her heart went out to him. She could understand having to carve a new life out for yourself when all you really wanted was your old one. It wasn't easy, but it had to be done. She knew she'd never be able to do it without the help of the Lord and Grandpa and Wade's family—Jake's family, too. Would he be willing to share them now that he was home?

Sara pulled in the drive and hurried into the house. It was time to start supper, and she couldn't worry about it now. She'd leave it all in the Lord's hands.

The mouth-watering smell of homemade stew greeted her as she entered the kitchen. Her grandfather turned from checking on a pan of cornbread in the oven.

"Grandpa, I'm sorry I'm late getting home."

"No problem, Darlin'. I was just waiting until you drove up to finish it up. Gave me something to do."

Sara hugged him and started setting the table. "I appreciate it, Grandpa. I would have been finished sooner, but I was at Gram's longer than I expected."

He nodded. "Ellie called a little while ago to see if you were back yet. She told me Jake and his baby girl are moving back." Grandpa took a seat at the table. "Said you two took to each other right off."

"Oh, Grandpa, she's adorable." Sara chuckled and told him about Meggie's lunch as she joined him at the table. "She grabbed hold of me and wouldn't let go. It felt so good to hold her. You know?"

Grandpa patted her hand. "Hindsight is always better than foresight. We erred on the side of caution, I guess, keeping babies and little ones away from you. We were just afraid it would be too painful, Sara."

"I know. But it was just what I needed."

Grandpa cleared his throat. "What about Jake? How does he seem?"

The timer went off, and Sara got up to take the cornbread out of the oven, glad for a minute or two to regroup. She placed the pan on a pad in the center of the table. "He's still struggling, I think."

"I guess he's been trying to deal with it all on his own. Maybe now he's home, we can help," Grandpa suggested.

Sara ladled the stew into bowls and brought them to the table while Grandpa cut the cornbread. Once they were seated again, he offered the blessing and asked the Lord to help them to help Jake in whatever way was needed.

"I hope he lets his family help him now that he's home," Sara said. "I can't imagine how hard the last year would have been on my own." She shook her head.

"Ellie said he's going to look for a house or build one in town."

"That's what she told me. He'll be staying with her for now. He seems a little concerned that Gram might not be up to keeping Meggie all day."

"Ellie? I don't think there's much that woman isn't up to."

"She's something, isn't she?"

"She sure is."

Something about the way he spoke made Sara look at her grandfather more closely. Could it be he was interested in

Gram? They both went to the seniors class at church on Tuesday mornings and served on several committees together. Was there romance in the air? Sara tried to stifle a small chuckle.

"What? Did you say something, Darlin'?"

She shook her head. "I was just agreeing with you."

The phone rang and Sara went to answer it, moaning inwardly at the sound of her mother-in-law's voice on the other end.

"Sara dear, did you get the teddy bears delivered safe and sound?" Nora asked.

Sara knew that wasn't the reason her mother-in-law had called, but she went along with it. "I did. They were a big hit too."

"That's good, Dear. I heard something today."

"Oh? What did you hear?" Nora was always on top of anything new that happened around town. She made it her business to know everyone else's. Sara admonished herself for her unkind thoughts, but they were true. Nora seemed to keep up with everyone and everything without having to leave the ranch.

"Jake is back in town."

"Yes, I know."

"Oh?"

"He came in while I was at Gram's picking up the bears she made."

"Humph. I guess he decided he needed some help with that child."

"That child's name is Meggie, Nora, and she's adorable. I'm sure Jake could use some help. He's had a great loss to deal with, as well as trying to be both mother and father to a baby." Sara was surprised at how defensive she sounded, but sometimes Nora's attitude really got to her.

"Well, yes, I guess it has been hard on him. But you've gotten through worse, Dear."

Sara looked up to see her grandfather watching her. She rolled her eyes, signaling that Nora was giving her opinion as always. "Was there anything else, Nora? We were eating dinner."

"Oh. Well, I wanted to see if you were free for lunch tomorrow."

The teddy bears were delivered. Sara couldn't come up with another excuse. She sighed silently. "Of course, Nora."

"Good. I'll meet you at Deana's at noon then. Unless you'd like me to pick you up?"

"No, I have some errands to run afterward. I'll just meet you there."

"All right, Dear. You have a good evening."

"You too, Nora."

Sara hung up and sat back down at the table. "I do care about Nora, Grandpa, I really do. And I know she's lonely. But sometimes she just makes me feel. . .smothered."

"Honey, you're a sweet and giving woman. But you're going to have to be careful that you don't let Nora try to run your life."

"She's already trying to do that, but I'm not going to let her. I just don't want to hurt her."

Grandpa got up to refill his bowl. "I know you don't, Sara, but she can't cling to you forever. You have your own life to get on with."

"I know." Somehow getting on with that life had seemed easier last night than it did right this minute.

☙

Meggie entertained everyone at supper that night. She grinned and cooed at her uncle Luke and cousin John. Jake held his breath, waiting for her to throw something at one of them, but she was on her best behavior.

"Look, look, did you see that grin she gave me?" Luke asked.

"She's a beauty, Jake," John said. "You'll have to beat the guys off with a stick when she gets to be a teenager."

"Hey, now. Let's not rush things." Jake watched as his daughter soaked up the attention like a sponge in water and knew he'd made the right decision in moving back. Meggie needed to know her family. Luke and John had fought over who got to hold her, feed her, and wipe her face ever since they'd gone upstairs with him to get her.

She'd been crying at the strange surroundings until Jake walked into the room. Then she'd given him that smile that always made his heart turn to mush, held out her arms to him, and said the most beautiful word in the world: "Dada." He'd lifted her out of her bed and gathered her close before turning to introduce her to her uncle and cousin.

When she'd seen Luke and John, she'd plopped her thumb in her mouth and laid her head on his shoulder, shy at first. But after they'd acted like a couple of two year olds trying to get her attention, she'd finally rewarded them each with a smile.

When Luke held out his hands to her and she went right to him, Jake felt much the same as he had when he saw her in Sara's arms. Abandoned. He shook the feeling off as he saw Luke's joy in holding his niece and Meggie's obvious love of the attention. That was why he had come back. For Meggie to have the family connections he'd grown up with. Now as he watched Luke, John, and Gram try to win his little girl's heart, he realized how much he'd missed being around his family. Resentment toward Wade flared up, and Jake worked to smother it. Wade was gone. What kind of person resented a dead man?

"All right!" John's exclamation brought Jake out of his thoughts.

After checking her cousin out all through supper, Meggie had finally lifted her arms to John. Jake cleaned her face and hands, unbuckled her highchair belt, and watched closely as John picked her up.

"I have held a baby before, Jake," John said, lifting Meggie out of the chair. "I know how to do this."

"Guess I'm a little overprotective," Jake admitted.

"Maybe just a little," John teased. "Now let me enjoy her. It took me long enough to get her to come to me."

"None of you have Sara's touch," Gram said. "Meggie took to her right off."

And they'd looked so natural and content; it'd made him almost jerk Meggie out of her arms. Jake couldn't shake the look in Sara's eyes out of his mind. He had to talk to her, try to explain that he hadn't known she'd lost her baby.

"We may not have a woman's touch, but we got Meggie to take to us, just the same," Luke said. "Let's take her into the living room and give her those toys we brought, John."

Jake followed them, glad for the diversion. "Going to spoil her already, are you?"

"That's what uncles and cousins are for, right, Gram?"

Chuckling, she joined them in the living room. "That's right, but Grammies get to spoil them most of all."

"Uh-oh, I can see I have a whole new set of problems moving back here."

Luke slapped him on the back. "You haven't seen anything yet, Brother."

❧

Sara remembered to call Gram before she started cleaning the kitchen. Her heart thudded with each ring. *Please, please don't let Jake answer the phone.* When Gram answered, Sara hoped her sigh of relief wasn't audible. She quickly told the older woman how well the teddy bears had gone over and asked how Meggie was settling in.

"She's having a great time, Sara. Luke and John came over and brought her some toys. I wish you could see all these grown men falling all over themselves trying to get that baby just to smile at them."

Sara laughed. "I bet that is a sight." She could hear exuberant noises in the background and wished she could see them all playing with Meggie.

"I think it's just what they both need. To be around family."

"I'm sure it is, Gram." It was a wonderful family and one she was proud to be part of, if only by marriage. She hoped she could stay close to them all with Jake back.

"Sara dear, I. . ."

"What is it, Gram?"

"Well, I told Jake about you losing the baby. We hadn't told him because of all he was going through at the time."

"It's all right, Gram. I understand."

"I think he feels real bad that he didn't know."

"There's no need for him to. Don't you worry about it."

"Well, you stop by anytime you need a baby to hold, you hear? And don't forget about Sunday night supper."

"Thanks, Gram. I will, and I won't forget. Grandpa wouldn't let me."

The older woman chuckled. "He'd better not. Good night, Dear."

"Night, Gram." Sara placed the receiver back on the phone and began cleaning the kitchen on autopilot. She was sure Gram was right that being around family would help Jake and Meggie. Melissa had had no living relatives, and the only family Meggie had was Jake's. That little girl needed to grow up being close to them. Everyone should know they had a family. Sara didn't know what she would have done after her parents died if it hadn't been for her grandparents taking her in and loving her.

She hoped being back with his family would take that haunted look from Jake's eyes. He looked so lost and alone. She did the only thing she could do for him. She prayed. *Dear Lord, I don't pretend to know Jake's relationship with You, but please help him heal. Please let him and Meggie make a good life here. In Jesus' name. Amen.*

Sara put a pot of coffee on and sat down to call the rest of the women who had made teddy bears. Everyone was thrilled that the bears had gone over so well and promised to have more ready in a month.

She took coffee to Grandpa and joined him in watching a rerun of *Happy Days*.

"Did you remember to call Ellie?" Grandpa asked during a commercial.

"I did. She reminded me about Sunday night supper."

"Did you tell her we wouldn't miss it?"

"I didn't think I had to. I just told her *you* wouldn't let me forget it."

Grandpa chuckled. "You were right. I do look forward to her supper all week."

Was it the suppers or Gram's company that Grandpa looked forward to? Sara admitted to herself that she might worry if Grandpa showed signs of being sweet on any other woman. But she would only rejoice if those two dear people cared for one another. She was going to have to watch the two of them closely Sunday night.

When the sitcom was over, she went into the kitchen and made a batch of Grandpa's favorite cookies. He'd fixed supper for the two of them; the least she could do was keep the cookie jar filled. She wasn't surprised to see him enter the kitchen just as she took out the first sheet of chocolate chip cookies.

"Mmm, those sure smell good." He got a glass and poured them both a glass of milk. "You spoil me, Honey."

He took a bite of warm cookie. "You make them just like your grandmother did. That woman sure could cook."

"Yes, she could. Gram's a pretty good cook too."

Grandpa nodded. "She sure is. Good woman, Ellie."

Sara smiled. "She's one of the best."

"Watching a toddler is going to keep her hopping, that's for sure." Grandpa changed the subject. "But I know she's thrilled to have that baby close."

"She was glowing this afternoon. But I think this must have been a fairly sudden decision. Jake said he didn't give much notice. I'm sure if he'd been planning it for any length of time, he would have let the family know."

"Ellie would have said something if she'd known."

"Oh, I'm sure she would have. Having a baby around is going to be good for the whole family. You should have heard the laughter coming over the phone lines earlier. From what

Gram said, I think Meggie's uncle Luke and cousin John are already in love with her."

"I'll have to get over there to see her soon." He paused. "You're all right, aren't you, Honey? I mean with Jake coming back and all. . . ."

"Why wouldn't I be?"

"Well now, Darlin', I seem to remember you doing your share of crying over him years ago."

"That was a long time ago, Grandpa." Sara didn't want to tell him that since seeing Jake, those days seemed closer somehow. The night Jake had been late coming home to celebrate her birthday and had caught Wade trying to comfort her with a kiss had suddenly become very vivid. She could remember Jake yelling and accusing her and Wade of seeing each other behind his back. She'd tried to explain, but Jake wouldn't listen. He'd turned on his heel and walked out of her life.

She got up to take the next tray of cookies out of the oven and bent to kiss the top of Grandpa's head. "Don't worry about me. That was all a lifetime ago."

"I'm not going to worry. With all that you've come through this last year, I don't think there's much you can't handle now."

"Thank you, Grandpa." His vote of confidence buoyed her spirits. It was the way she'd felt when she'd left home this morning. Somehow with all that'd happened during the day she'd lost the joy she'd started out with.

Grandpa ate one more cookie and got to his feet. "I think I'll go up and read awhile. Don't you stay up too late, you hear? You'll need all your wits about you for that lunch with Nora tomorrow." He chuckled as he headed out of the room.

Sara couldn't stop herself from joining in. He was right. Tomorrow would definitely be a challenge. "Night, Grandpa. I love you."

"Love you too, Darlin'."

Sara took the last batch of cookies from the oven, washed the baking dishes, and put everything away. She was still too keyed up to call it a night and decided to enjoy the early spring weather once more. As she opened the front door, her feet suddenly froze in place. Her hand flew to her throat.

Jake was standing there, his Stetson in one hand and the other raised to knock at the door. "Sara, I'm sorry. I didn't mean to frighten you. I saw your lights on and. . .um, could we talk a minute?"

Sara released the breath she'd been holding. "Of course. Would you like to come in?" Her heart did a tap dance. What did he want to talk about?

"No, that's all right. I won't take much of your time." He took a step back and leaned against the porch rail, crossing his booted feet.

Sara slipped outside and leaned back against the screen door. Did he feel as tense around her as she did near him? The silence thickened until she could stand it no longer. "Are Gram and Meggie all right? Nothing is wrong, is it?"

"They're fine. Gram was watching the news when I left, and Meggie is asleep. For the night, I hope. Meggie loves all the attention she's been getting, but everything is new to her."

"Your family will help her adjust to the move in no time, Jake. They're wonderful—I don't know what I would have done without them." Something inside her whispered it was Jake who needed them badly now.

"Yeah, they are. Except they didn't tell me. . . ." He looked down at his feet and back up again before his brown gaze settled on her face. "Sara, I'm sorry for appearing so unfeeling this afternoon. I didn't know about the baby you lost. I'm so very sorry. . . ."

"Jake, it's all right," she said softly. "You had your own pain to deal with. This evening Gram told me that they hadn't told you."

"I wish I'd known."

Sara nodded. She could hear the sincerity in his voice. "I know."

"Wishing doesn't change much, does it?"

She knew he was talking about more than the fact that no

one had told him about her baby. "No, it doesn't."

Jake looked as though he was going to reach out to her, but then he straightened and turned to go. He cleared his throat and turned back to face her once more. "Guess I'd better get back. Meggie may wake up and be frightened in a new place and all."

"Okay." The awkwardness between them squeezed at Sara's heart. "Thank you, Jake."

He put his hat back on and tipped it slightly before he turned and headed down the steps.

Sara watched him walk to his car, and something about his slumped shoulders reached out to her. The sorrow surrounding him was almost tangible. Her heart went out to him, for she knew the feeling well. But she knew where to turn when those moments of utter misery threatened to drown her. Tears gathered in her eyes. *Dear Lord, please help Jake the way You've helped me.*

She turned to go back inside. Sitting out in the cool night air no longer held any appeal. She'd only think about other times she'd sat on this same porch, in that same porch swing. . .with Jake.

She wasn't going to let herself think about the past. No, about the bad times—or the good. No, she wasn't ready to dredge it all up. Jake was right: Wishing wouldn't change a thing.

three

Jake looked down at his sleeping daughter. Dark hair curled around her little face. Every few seconds, she sucked the tiny thumb in her mouth. The other hand clutched a stuffed toy. Her soft, even breathing was music to his ears. He could not imagine life without Meggie. How did Sara find the strength to go on day after day? She seemed to have come to terms with it all, but he didn't know how.

He covered Meggie up and quietly left the room, leaving a nightlight glowing and keeping the door cracked. Making his way downstairs, he let himself out the front door. Gram had gone up to bed shortly after he'd returned from Sara's. He didn't tell her where he'd gone, but he suspected she knew.

Jake lowered himself onto the porch steps and leaned back to look at the starry sky. He thought he'd feel better after apologizing to Sara, but he'd been wrong. Seeing her on the same front porch where they'd spent so much time only brought back memories best left buried.

But how was he going to keep such thoughts at bay now that they lived in the same town again? He hoped they didn't run into each other at every turn. How could he have forgotten that she was now a part of his extended family? Jake ran his fingers through his hair. Had he just blocked out all thoughts of Sara? Had that made it all easier on him?

A deep sigh escaped him. He shook his head and groaned. She'd looked wonderful tonight. Tendrils of hair had escaped from her french braid, making him want to reach out and curl a wisp around his finger the way he used to. He'd had to catch himself to keep from doing just that. And her eyes. How could eyes reflect such deep sadness and serenity at the same time?

There was a quiet peace about Sara that he wished he could

find for himself. He would have liked to ask her about how she'd reached that point in her life, but he couldn't. There was a time he could have asked her anything, but not now. He'd felt so awkward around her; he could barely get out the few sentences he'd gone there to say.

Jake got to his feet. Maybe he should have waited for another day to talk to her, but he wouldn't have been able to sleep. He knew he'd changed a lot, but he couldn't live with the idea that she thought him totally insensitive after this afternoon.

Making sure the door was locked, he turned out the lights and headed for bed. Tomorrow he was going to call a Realtor. The sooner he decided whether to buy or build, the sooner he and Meggie would be in their own home. And the less likely he'd be to run into Sara.

❧

Sara glanced at her watch as she parked her car on Main Street. She'd gotten off to a slow start that morning and was going to be late for her lunch with Nora. Her mother-in-law hated tardiness, but it couldn't be helped.

She'd tossed and turned most of the night. Jake's return had shaken her, no doubt about it. There'd been a time when they could talk about anything. But that was then, and this was now, and nothing was going to change that fact. Still, she wished she didn't feel so on edge around him.

The tinkling bell above the door announced her arrival at the diner. Sara spotted Nora sitting in a booth and checking the time on her watch. She hurried over and quickly slipped into the seat across from her mother-in-law.

"I'm sorry I'm late, Nora. I didn't sleep well last night, and I just couldn't get going this morning."

She was rewarded with a half smile. "It's all right, Dear. Was there any particular reason you had trouble sleeping? You aren't coming down with a cold, are you?"

"No, I don't think so. I guess I was just too tired." Or too keyed up after Jake's visit. But she wasn't going to tell Nora that. She grabbed a menu and scanned the lunch specials.

"Well, you do keep yourself quite busy these days. You haven't been out to the ranch in several weeks."

Sara took a deep breath and smiled at her mother-in-law. "I'm sorry I haven't made it out there lately, Nora."

Sara was relieved when the waitress came to take their order, but she realized it was only a short reprieve.

The waitress had no more than turned her back when Nora got to the heart of the matter. "I really do wish you would move back to the ranch, Sara."

"And I wish you'd just move into town." Sara caught her breath as soon as the words left her mouth. She couldn't believe she'd actually said them out loud. She was just so weary of this conversation.

Nora sat up straighter and inhaled sharply. "Why would I want to do that? I have a perfectly beautiful home at the ranch. I can come into town whenever I feel like it, but the ranch is my home."

Sara nodded, knowing she should have kept quiet. "I just thought you might be happier here. There's more to do, you could see more of your friends—"

"I'm perfectly happy at the ranch. It's where I raised Wade. I don't want to move."

Sara reached over and patted Nora's hand. "My point exactly. I can understand that, Nora. I don't want to move, either," she said softly.

Nora jerked her hand from underneath Sara's. She took a sip of coffee and brushed at crumbs only she could see. "I see."

"I hope you do. Nora, you know you'll always be family to me. You've been wonderful to me, and I love you. But Grandpa isn't getting any younger, and I want to be close by. It will be much easier on me when I resume teaching in the fall if I'm living in town. I—"

"There is no need for you to teach. Wade never wanted you to work, Sara. If you invest what he left you, you shouldn't need to work."

"Nora, I want to teach. When Wade was alive, I loved being his wife, but I never felt I had enough to do then, and I need to keep busy. I can't just sit around—"

"Like I do. Is that what you're saying?"

"Nora, no! I—"

A look from Nora silenced her as the waitress approached with their lunch. Sara was torn between relief and frustration when Nora changed the subject as soon as the waitress left the table.

"What are you bringing to Ellie's Sunday night?" Nora asked.

Caught off guard, Sara didn't want to tell her that she was trying to think of a way to avoid going to the regular Sunday night supper at Gram's. For as long as she could remember, Gram had invited family and friends to her home for supper after church on Sunday nights. But now, with Jake back in town, Sara felt the need to bow out. "I'm not sure."

"I think I'll have Cook bake one of her famous chile casseroles." Nora took a bite of her chicken-salad sandwich and chewed delicately.

Sara's appetite was diminishing rapidly as she thought about not being able to spend as much time with family as she liked. But the only way to avoid seeing Jake would be to distance herself from the whole family. It was his family, after all. She picked at the salad she'd ordered and tried not to think about it.

The bell over the door of the diner jingled several times, but it wasn't until she saw Nora's face flush that Sara took notice of who'd entered.

Luke Breland was striding over to the booth, with Jake slowly coming up behind him. Sara's heart started hammering in her chest.

"Aunt Nora, Sara! It's good to see you both." Luke gave them each a kiss on the cheek and motioned to Jake. "Look who showed up on Gram's doorstep yesterday."

The smile Nora gave Luke disappeared when she looked

at Jake. "Jacob, I heard you were back in town with your daughter."

Jake looked irritated but bent to brush his lips across his aunt's cheek. "It's good to see you too, Aunt Nora."

Nora's face flushed at his slight admonition. "You decided you needed help, did you, Jacob?"

Sara was appalled at Nora's rudeness. "We all need help from time to time, Nora. I've had to have a lot of that myself."

"I decided it was time Meggie got to know her family," Jake said gruffly.

"Well, I just hope watching her isn't too much for Ellie. She's not getting any younger, you know." Nora calmly took a sip of her iced tea.

Sara couldn't believe Nora was treating Jake so badly. "Nora, you know Gram loves babies. And there are plenty of people around to help out if she needs it."

"Including you, I suppose?"

"Of course, including me." Sara couldn't resist adding, "And you too, Nora. After all, Meggie is your great-niece. I'm sure you'd be willing to step in if Gram needed you."

Nora coughed, almost choking on her tea, and Luke patted her on the back.

"Don't worry, Aunt Nora," Jake said. "I don't think you or Sara will be needed. I'm fully capable of taking care of my own daughter. And I'm sure John would understand if I worked at home."

He clapped Luke on the shoulder. "Speaking of work, we'd better get those sandwiches we ordered and get back to it. I'll go see if Deana has them ready."

Sara watched him walk away and willed her heartbeat to return to normal. She looked up to see Luke smiling down at her.

"Thanks for the offer to help Gram with Meggie, Sara. I know it wasn't easy for Jake to realize he needed to come home. I sure don't want him feeling like he's putting Gram out."

"I'm sure Gram's loving every minute of it." Sara smiled

back at Luke. "But I'll check on her later to make sure she's all right."

Luke bent and kissed her cheek once more. "Thanks, Sara. Good-bye, Aunt Nora." He joined Jake at the door, and they left without so much as a backward glance from Jake.

"Humph! That boy has a lot of nerve coming back here," Nora said as soon as the two men were outside.

"Nora! What is your problem with Jake? He's your nephew!" Sara might not be happy that she was going to run into him at every turn, but he had a right to make his home here as much as she or anyone else did.

"How can you defend his coming back home and just dumping his daughter on Ellie?" Nora asked stiffly.

"Nora, Sweet Springs is his hometown. And I saw Gram with Meggie yesterday. I can assure you, she doesn't feel dumped upon!" Sara looked up in time to catch Nora dabbing at her eyes with a tissue and immediately felt bad for upsetting her.

"I'm sorry, Nora. But it's not like you to be rude to people." At least not to their face, Sara thought. Nora's technique was usually much more subtle.

"I just think he's made a mistake. He's going to let everyone get used to having the baby around and then he'll decide he wants to move back to Albuquerque."

While Nora's reasoning sounded logical, Sara felt that the woman was reaching for any reason to excuse her attitude toward Jake.

"I'm sure they will just be glad for whatever time they have with Meggie. She's delightful."

"Yes. . .I'm sure she is," Nora said, sounding wistful.

Sara immediately felt ashamed of herself for being critical. Although Nora had never seemed that excited about the prospect of becoming a grandmother, Sara was sure her mother-in-law would have loved the baby had it lived. Her heart knotted in pain at the losses they'd both suffered. "Nora, I—"

"I'm sorry, Dear, but I really have to leave. I have a doctor's appointment," Nora said, easing out of the booth.

"You aren't sick, are you?" Sara asked, feeling even worse.

"Just a checkup. Since Doc Edwards married Hilda and retired, I haven't bothered to find a new doctor. But several people have told me that the new doctor in town is good, and you never know when you might need medical care. So I made an appointment. If I think he's any good, I'll have Doc's office send my records to him," she explained, pulling a wad of bills from her purse and laying them on the table. "That should take care of lunch. If not, I'll pay you later."

Sara stood and gave Nora the quick, impersonal hug she seemed to expect but not like. So much for having a nice, calm lunch with Nora, she thought as she watched the woman hurry out the door. She sat back down and pushed what was left of her salad away. What little appetite she'd managed to hold on to was now totally gone.

"Sara, you look like you could use a friend and a fresh cup of coffee." Deana stood with the coffeepot in one hand, two cups in the other, and a smile on her face.

Sara summoned up a smile of her own. She and Deana had been good friends since high school, and Deana could read her all too well. "You couldn't be more right. Can you join me?"

Deana glanced around the diner and motioned to the waitress that she was taking a break. She slid into the side of the booth Nora had vacated, pushed aside the empty plate, and poured them both some coffee.

"Mmm. Feels good just to sit down. Some days I wish Mom hadn't given me this diner when she got married. I have a whole new respect for that woman, though. She raised us all by working really, really hard. I never realized just how tough it was to run this place until I took over." Deana took a sip of coffee.

"Have you heard from her and Doc lately?"

Deana nodded. "They're camping up in Colorado. She said

they'd be coming home in a week or two. I'm ready. I miss them when they're gone months at a time."

Sara nodded and stirred her tea.

"But I didn't take this break to talk about Mom and Doc."

"No?"

"No. I came because you're looking a little forlorn. And I want you to tell Aunty Deana what has you so down in the dumps."

Sara chuckled and shrugged. "A little of this, a little of that. I was curt with Nora because she was rude to Jake, and now I feel bad. I don't know why I felt I needed to take up for him anyway."

"Maybe because it was the right thing to do?" Deana propped her chin in her hand and waited for Sara to answer.

"He just looks so. . .adrift, you know? And I don't know why Nora seems to get so edgy when his name is brought up. But then I got to thinking that maybe it has something to do with his child being all right, while I lost her grandchild."

"Now that kind of thinking is bound to make you feel bad. Quit looking for excuses for Nora's rudeness, my friend. Far as I can tell, she's never needed a reason to be rude. She just is."

Sara tried but failed to contain the chuckle that erupted.

Deana laughed along with her. "Now that's more like it. Don't you let Nora make you feel bad, Sara."

Sara sighed. "I just don't like to upset her."

"Honey, anyone who doesn't think like Nora or agree with everything she says and isn't at her beck and call upsets that woman. You of all people should know that by now."

"But she's so lonely. And. . .I still feel it was—"

"Sara, the wreck was *not* your fault. You were pregnant. You had a craving for ice cream at ten o'clock at night. You and Wade went to get some. Thousands of expectant parents do the exact same thing every night."

"I know, Deana. I really do know that. It's just that Wade was Nora's only son, and now that he's gone, I feel responsible for her. But she wants me to move back out to the ranch, and I just can't do that."

"Nor should you. Nora can't live your life for you, or hers through you. You are here for her, you care about her, but you have to get on with your life. Personally I never knew how you stood living out there with her when Wade was alive. I don't think I could have done it."

Sara was relieved when the bell on the door jangled, announcing more customers. She didn't want to lie and say it'd been easy living at the ranch, but she didn't want to sound disloyal to her husband's mother, either.

Deana sighed and slid out of the booth. "Break's over. Got to get back to the kitchen."

Sara gathered her purse and prepared to leave. "You take it easy, Deana. I'll talk to you later." She paid the waitress and headed out the door to her car.

So far the day wasn't going as planned. The lunch with Nora had been anything but calming. . .especially after Jake and Luke came into the diner. Sara still couldn't believe how protective of Jake she'd felt. Nora had no reason to be so rude to him. He was her nephew, and he'd suffered a loss in the past year too. How could she have acted so unfeeling toward him?

And why do I feel I have to take up for him at every turn? He's a grown man and perfectly capable of fighting his own battles. He could probably hold his own with Nora better than I could, anyway.

Sara pulled out of the parking space and headed for the grocery store. It was just that he seemed so unlike the Jake she used to know. He was so serious and aloof. And there was a look in his eyes that Sara couldn't name or forget. *O Lord, he needs You so much. Please ease his pain. Little Meggie needs him to be the happy, loving person he used to be.*

Sara sighed as she pulled into the parking lot of the grocery store. She wanted to help Jake, she really did. But all she could do was pray for him, knowing the Lord would listen.

❧

Jake took the last bite of his cheeseburger and crumpled up

the sack it'd come in. He aimed and threw, hitting the trash can at the side of John's desk.

"Good shot!" Luke whistled. "You been practicing trash ball a lot, Brother?"

Jake chuckled and shook his head. "I was aiming for Aunt Nora's backside. That woman never has liked me."

John laughed. "Aunt Nora? What did she do now?"

"She was in Deana's when we went to pick up lunch." Luke crumpled his own bag and threw it away. "Wasn't too nice to Jake. Downright mean, if you ask me." He leaned back in one of two leather chairs facing John's desk.

"Nora never has been known for her sweetness."

"I shouldn't let her bother me," Jake explained, "but she made it sound like I just dumped Meggie in Gram's lap." He sat down in the empty chair and raked his fingers through his hair.

"Sara took up for you, though," Luke said. "And we all know Gram can speak for herself. She'll let you know if it's too much for her."

"Sara took up for you?" John whistled. "She rarely takes up for herself around Nora."

"Good thing she moved back in with her granddad after Wade died," Luke added. "Nora would love to call all the shots in Sara's life now." He stood and stretched. "I've got to get back to the ranch, boys. Uncle Ben should be calling me to let me know about the new livestock he bought. Let me know if there's anything I can do to help you get settled in, Jake. It's good to have you home, no matter how Aunt Nora feels about you." He chuckled on his way out the door.

John turned to Jake. "It is good to have you back. Don't you let Nora bother you."

"No, I won't," Jake assured his cousin. "I do want to make sure taking care of Meggie isn't too much for Gram, though. Mind if I take off early? I need to pick up some things at the store for Meggie, and—"

"Jake, you can take all the time you need. I'm just glad you finally agreed to come into practice with me. But there's no hurry. Get your bearings; get sweet Meggie settled in. If you feel you have to, you can take some files home to familiarize yourself with our clients, but you'll get to know them all soon enough. If you hadn't agreed to move back, I'd still be handling it all myself, anyway."

Jake nodded. Maybe he had been in too big a hurry to start working with John. There was no reason he couldn't get Meggie settled in a little better before he started working. "Thanks, John. I think I could use a little time to adjust to being back. And I don't want anyone thinking I can't take care of my own child."

John joined him at the door of the office and slapped him on the back. "Jake, no one is going to think that. After all, you've been taking care of her real well since Melissa's death. You turned down all kinds of help then. Don't let Aunt Nora get to you."

"Thanks, Cousin." Jake felt his tension begin to ease. "It's good to be home."

"And even better to have you here. Kiss Meggie for me."

Jake nodded and grinned. "Now that I can do."

❧

Sara pulled out the list she'd made that morning and grabbed a buggy. She wanted to make Grandpa his favorite meal as a way of thanking him for just being there. If he hadn't owned a home in this town, would she still be out at the ranch, living under Nora's thumbnail? Sara did care about Wade's mother, but there was no way she could live with her, and she hoped Nora would stop asking after today.

Sara's mood improved quickly once she was in the store and running into first one and then another smiling face. Mrs. Mead gushed about how happy she was the bears had been a hit and thanked Sara for coming up with the idea. Ida Connors hadn't helped with the bears the first time around, but after hearing how well they went over, she offered to help with the next batch.

Sara had put the lunchtime episode out of her mind by the time she'd picked up the ingredients for the meatloaf. Smiling, she turned down the next aisle and headed to the checkout lane, picturing the smile on Grandpa's face when he saw what was for supper. She would have plowed right into Jake's buggy if he hadn't swerved to the other side of the aisle.

Sara's hand flew to her mouth as she realized she'd almost hit him. "Jake! I'm sorry. Obviously I wasn't looking where I was going."

"It's all right, Sara. I looked up just in time. We seem to be running into each other today."

Sara noticed the buggy was full of disposable diapers and an assortment of baby food and snacks. There was something endearing about such a masculine man shopping for a baby with ease. "Is Meggie settling in all right? I was going to check on her and Gram this afternoon."

"She's settling in fine. And there's no need for you to check on them. John and I decided to slow down my return to work for a little while, so you can assure Nora that I won't be taking advantage of Gram."

"Jake, I—"

"I'm sorry, Sara. That was uncalled for. I guess I'm still stinging from Nora's remarks. Thank you for. . .coming to my defense earlier."

Sara nodded and tried to hide the sudden hurt she felt that he obviously didn't want her helping Gram with Meggie. It was probably for the best, but it still stung. "It's all right, Jake. I'm sorry Nora was so rude."

"It's not your fault. I hope she didn't give you too hard a time about taking up for me."

"She'll get over it." Sara saw the first hint of a smile from Jake.

"That's what I figured," he said. "But I don't want to give her anything to fuel that tongue of hers. I'm going to make this my home again whether she's happy about it or not."

"I know the family is glad to have you home, Jake. Gram is

thrilled." She just wished she didn't feel so unsure of herself around him. It was a feeling that seemed to deepen each time she saw him.

"I want Meggie to know her family," Jake continued.

"She should. It's a good family to know."

Jake nodded. "Yes, it is."

Sara didn't know what to say next.

Jake found his voice first. "I'd better get going and let you finish your shopping."

Sara was almost relieved to be able to put her cart in motion. "I do need to get supper started. Tell Gram I said hi and give Meggie an extra hug for me."

"I will."

"Bye, Jake."

"Bye, Sara," Jake said as he rounded the corner.

Sara paid for her purchases and headed for her car. No, life wasn't going to get any easier with Jake back in town.

four

Sara crumbled crackers, chopped onion and bell pepper, and grated carrots, while trying to banish thoughts of Jake from her mind. Adding some of each ingredient a little at a time, she mixed them with a combination of ground beef and bulk sausage before adding the seasonings, eggs, and tomato soup. She was concentrating so hard on keeping her thoughts off Jake, she didn't hear Grandpa slip up behind her.

"Smells good in here already." He looked over her shoulder. "Meatloaf! How did you know that's what I've been hungry for?"

She had to chuckle. "It was a pretty good guess. You're always hungry for meatloaf, Grandpa."

"Just yours, Honey. You make it just like your grandmother did. But I have to admit, I like yours even better with that cheese you tuck inside."

"Thanks. That's quite a compliment." Sara continued to mold the mixture into a loaf, leaving some to the side and hollowing out the center. She then filled it with grated cheese and covered it with the remaining meat mixture. Grandpa was right. It did smell good even before it was cooked.

Sara slid the loaf pan into the oven and added two foil-wrapped potatoes alongside the pan, before turning to her grandfather. "Should be ready in about an hour. Want a glass of iced tea? We could sit out on the porch for awhile."

"Sounds good to me," Grandpa said. But he turned her toward the door. "You go on out and I'll bring the tea. You look a little frazzled."

"Am I that obvious?" At her grandfather's grin, she shrugged and chuckled. "Okay, I'll meet you out front."

Setting the swing in motion, Sara closed her eyes and

tried to relax as she swung back and forth. She was going to have to learn how to deal with an unhappy Nora *and* with running into Jake again. She simply had no choice in the matter.

She prayed silently, asking the Lord to help her deal with the changes that Jake's return would cause. Sara knew the Lord would help her through it all. She just had to give it over to Him. With the acknowledgment that He still was in control, the tension she'd felt all afternoon began to drain away.

"You had lunch with Nora, didn't you? Is that what had you uptight?" Grandpa asked as he let the screen door slam behind him. He handed her a glass of tea and sat down in the wicker rocker across from the swing.

Sara nodded. "It sure contributed to it. I upset her, and I didn't want to." She took a sip of tea.

"Oh? Want to tell me about it?" He settled back in the rocker.

"Jake and Luke came in while we were there, and Nora was just plain rude to Jake. She practically accused him of dumping Meggie on Gram, and I found myself taking up for him."

"No!" Grandpa shook his head and chuckled. "Nora probably wasn't too happy about that."

"Especially not after I'd told her I didn't want to move to the ranch."

"Well, Darlin', you did the right thing on both counts. You don't want to move back to the ranch, and she shouldn't have been rude to Jake."

"I even found myself offering to help, if Meggie got to be too much for Gram."

"I'm glad to hear it, Darlin'. I went to see Ellie today. You were right. Meggie is adorable. And she's a handful." He smiled. "She kept us both busy until Jake showed up."

"I think he's afraid she might be too much for Gram."

Grandpa leaned back and started rocking. "Well, Ellie isn't going to admit that she might be, but I'm sure relieved that Jake isn't going to work full time, just yet. I'm afraid keeping

Meggie on an everyday basis might just be a little too hard for her."

He shook his head and grinned. "She's pulling up to everything, trying to walk. Ellie says she can say a few words, too. She's something, that Meggie is."

"Yes, she certainly is." Remembering how wonderful it felt to hold Meggie in her arms, Sara almost wished Jake hadn't decided to take his time settling into the law practice. She'd have loved to help with the baby. But it wouldn't matter. Jake had made it perfectly clear that he didn't want her help.

❧

"Jake, don't you take anything Nora says to heart," Gram declared. "Meggie and I will be just fine. And there are plenty of people around to help me, if I need them to." She poured them both some coffee and sat down at the table, where they watched Meggie stack blocks in a playpen set up by the back door. "That woman just doesn't know how to mind her own business."

Jake had to chuckle. "Gram, that woman is your daughter-in-law."

"I know. She wasn't always this way. Nora's turned bitter over the years since Mark was killed in Vietnam." Gram sighed and shook her head. "It's sad. The Nora he married was a kind and caring woman. Just don't you let her get to you."

"Don't worry. I'm determined not to let her bother me. I just don't want anyone else thinking that I've come home to dump Meggie on my family."

"Did Will make you feel that way before he left here?"

"No, he didn't." In fact, Sara's grandfather had been very nice, welcoming him back to Sweet Springs.

"And no one else, except Nora, is going to, either. Jake, you're being too hard on yourself. The whole town knows you've been taking care of Meggie ever since Melissa's death—and that you turned down repeated offers of help."

Jake leaned back in his chair and rubbed the back of his neck. "Actually, I think taking a break and getting settled will help both me and Meggie. The move is bound to unsettle her, and I'd like to make it as easy as I can on her."

"Jake, as long as you are in her life, that baby doesn't care where she lives. Children adjust much easier than we adults do. Take the break if you think it will do you some good. Just don't do it on my account."

Jake tried not to smile. His grandmother would never change. She wasn't about to admit that watching Meggie might be too much for her. But looking closely at her, there was no denying the fact that she looked plumb tuckered out.

"I thought I'd bring some of the files home and go over them here so that I'm familiar with our clients when I do start working full time with John. And I can contact a realtor. If I don't find a house I like, I'll just look into building one."

"You know you are welcome to live here as long as you need to."

"I know that, Gram. And I thank you. But the sooner I find Meggie and me a place of our own, the easier it will be to make Sweet Springs home again." He knew he'd made the right decision in coming back, but there were some things he was going to have to work at getting used to. Like running into Sara when he least expected it. And he hadn't expected it today. Not at the diner and especially not at the grocery store.

"Sara offered to help if you needed her. I think that upset Nora even more than my presence did. She looked like she'd sucked on a sour lemon."

Ellie shook her head. "You know, she's going to have to start living her own life one of these days."

"Sara?"

"No, Nora. Sara will get on with hers in time. She's young. But Nora seems to delight in trying to run everyone's life but her own."

"Luke and John said it took a lot for Sara to stand up to her today. Why is that? She's Wade's widow. She doesn't owe Nora anything."

"No, she doesn't. But Sara doesn't want to hurt her, either,

Jake. Nora has clung to her since Wade's death, and Sara feels she's all Nora has left of Wade."

Wade. Jake wondered if he'd ever get over resenting the man who won Sara's heart. Chair legs scraped the kitchen floor as Jake got to his feet and tried to bury the past once more. He bent to pick Meggie up and cuddle her.

"Jake?"

He turned his attention back to his grandmother. "Yes, Ma'am?"

"Wade's gone. You're going to have to come to terms with the past. You know things aren't always what they seem."

"I don't have time to think about the past, Gram." He blew kisses on the back of Meggie's neck to hear her giggle. "Making a new life for myself and Meggie is about all I can handle right now. We're going to go play in the backyard. Why don't you take a nap before supper? I'll cook tonight. I can cook, you know."

"Humph! Jake Breland, I've never been a nap taker and I'm not about to take one at five-thirty in the afternoon. I wouldn't sleep a wink tonight. And I'm not ready to turn my kitchen over to anyone, either." Gram got up from the table and walked over to the refrigerator. "I'll call you when supper is ready."

Jake hoisted Meggie onto his hip and headed outside. "Come on, Sugar. I think we've been dismissed."

૨ૐ

Sara had just been congratulating herself for managing not to run into Jake for the last several days—until Lydia, John's mother, called inviting her to a welcome home cookout for Jake.

"I'm not sure, Lydia, I—"

"You don't have a thing that's pressing, and you know it, Sara. Now be a good girl and say you'll come. You don't get out enough, and besides, I'm not taking no for an answer."

Sara sighed. She knew Lydia meant what she said. She'd been after Sara to get out more for months. Besides, there'd be too many questions from the family if she didn't go. "I'll be there. Can I bring anything?"

"Just yourself and Will. We're just having hamburgers and hotdogs. And dessert, of course."

"Grandpa will love that."

"You'll both have a good time, you'll see."

Sure we will, Sara thought as she said good-bye and hung up the phone. She'd spent the last few days helping Grandpa with weeding and watering his garden. And she'd done some serious spring cleaning. . .anything to keep from going out and possibly running into Jake again. Seeing him only confused her.

This was the man who'd hurt her all those years ago by dumping her and then marrying Melissa several months later. Why did she feel this strong need to reach out to him now? He just looked so lost and alone the few times she'd seen him. He should be the last person she was thinking of, but she'd thought of little else since his return.

She'd wanted to call Gram and see how Meggie was doing several times during the day, but she'd been afraid Jake would answer the phone. Part of her resented the fact that she no longer felt she could just pick up the phone and call whenever she wanted to, and the other part of her wanted to take the easy way out by staying away. Seeing Jake wasn't easy, it wasn't easy at all.

Well, Lydia had taken care of all her good intentions. Now she'd have to show up or have everyone upset that she didn't.

Sara poured a glass of iced tea and took it outside. She'd asked Grandpa to take a pot of soup and a batch of cookies she'd made over to Gram's for her. She felt she was helping in some way by seeing to it that Gram had a break from cooking a meal here and there. And this way she'd get news of Meggie when he got home.

She just wished she'd get past this overwhelming urge to hold Meggie again. Tears threatened to well up, and Sara forced them back down. She wasn't going to cry. She wasn't going to let herself. She'd spent the better part of a year crying over her loss, and she wasn't about to start crying over what might have been.

She had to get up and get busy doing something, anything to get her mind off the past. She'd get dressed and go shopping, that's what she'd do. Maybe buying something new to wear to Lydia's party would get her out of her doldrums. It'd be fun, and surely Jake wouldn't be shopping in a ladies' dress shop.

Half an hour later, Sara came out of the dressing room wearing a colorful sundress. Catching a glimpse of someone, she sighed. This day wasn't getting any better. While Jake wasn't in the shop, Nora was.

"Sara dear. I thought that was your car outside. If I'd known you were going shopping, I'd have asked you to come with me. We could have had lunch together." Nora's gaze took in the long dress Sara had on. "That's a little bright for you, don't you think?"

It was better to laugh than cry, Sara thought as she chuckled. "I like it, Nora. It feels cool and summery."

"Are you buying it for anything special?"

"Lydia is throwing a party—"

"Yes, for Jake. I was invited too."

"Oh? And you're shopping for something new, too. That's nice, Nora."

"No. I am not buying anything new for that party. I really hadn't planned on going. I just saw your car outside and thought I'd stop in and see you."

"That was nice of you, Nora. The shopping trip was just spur of the moment. I haven't bought anything new in a long time." Not since she'd bought her maternity clothes. Nora had been with her that day and insisted on buying several outfits for her. They'd had a very good time. Sara had forgotten how excited about the baby Nora had been. Now she wondered if the sadness in Nora's eyes was reflected in her own.

Sara forced herself to put thoughts of the past away. She couldn't let herself start thinking about the pain of the last year. She'd come too far. But still, she felt some of the weight of Nora's sadness. "Why don't you come have supper with me and Grandpa?"

"No, Dear. I have some errands to run. I'll leave you to your shopping." Nora pulled the shoulder strap of her handbag higher up and turned to leave. "I'll see you tomorrow night, though."

"Oh, good. You've changed your mind? You're going to go? Lydia will be so—"

Nora was out the door before Sara finished the sentence. Sara sighed and headed back to the dressing room. She wasn't making Nora very happy these days.

By the time the next evening rolled around, Sara wanted nothing more than to get out of going to the party for Jake, but Grandpa was excited about it. She dressed in the colorful dress she'd bought the day before and joined him downstairs.

"You look beautiful, Darlin'. It's time we had a party around here. You need a change of scenery."

Sara forced herself to smile. Grandpa loved parties, and she wasn't about to spoil his fun. "Thank you. You don't look too bad yourself. And you smell really good. You trying to impress anyone I know, Grandpa?"

"Just Meggie." He chuckled. "You know that little tyke has been playing hard to get. Won't let me hold her at all."

Mention of the baby's name made Sara realize how she was hoping to see her tonight.

❧

Jake took a deep breath as he followed Ellie up the walk. "Be a sweetie tonight, Meggie, and help me through this," he whispered in the baby's ear.

He hadn't wanted a fuss made over his coming home, but he didn't want to hurt Aunt Lydia and Uncle Ben, so here he was. He'd dreaded it all day. But there was no getting out of it. He just hoped that everyone was so enthralled with his daughter that he could blend into the background.

John answered the door and took Meggie and her diaper bag. Meggie was quite happy with all the attention, and Jake had to force himself not to take her back. Luke came up and led him away before he could protest.

"Meggie will be just fine, Jake. If she starts crying, you can rest assured John will find you."

By the time they'd made their way outside, Jake felt like he'd greeted most of Sweet Springs. Everyone was very nice and seemed genuinely pleased that he was back. He spotted Nora holding court, seated in a chaise across the yard, and was thankful that he didn't have to speak to her just yet. What was she doing here anyway? He knew she wasn't here to welcome him home. Run him out on the rails would be more like it.

Just then Aunt Lydia and Uncle Ben rushed up to him and welcomed him home. Lydia wanted to know where Meggie was and immediately went inside to look for her.

Luke helped to nudge Jake's memory by putting names to faces of old classmates and friends who came up to him, and after awhile, Jake began to relax and have a good time. But it wasn't until he spotted Will and Sara coming out the back door that he knew in spite of the past, in spite of trying to block thoughts of her out of his mind, in spite of the fact that she should be the last person he wanted to see, he'd been waiting to see if she would be here, all along. She looked out across the yard and her eyes met his. Sara smiled, and he was struck once more by the peaceful serenity in her eyes. She'd come to terms with the pain she'd suffered, but he didn't know how.

She looked wonderful. Her auburn hair was caught up on top of her head, and she was in an aqua and yellow sundress that looked wonderful on her. He knew from the way family and friends alike greeted her that Sara was special to everyone here. There was no getting around it. As much as he felt he needed to stay away from her, she was a part of his family and this town. Oh yes, he was going to have to find a way to deal with the fact that he was drawn to Sara as much now as he ever had been in the past.

❧

Sara was glad so many people turned out for Jake's party,

especially after the way Nora had treated him in the diner. When she glanced up and caught Jake looking at her, she smiled and her heart seemed to somersault all the way to her stomach when he smiled back. For a moment she wished she could change the past and go back to the time when they'd been best friends and shared everything—

"You look lovely, Dear," Nora said, appearing from nowhere. "I wish Wade were here to see you."

Looking into the cool blue eyes of her mother-in-law, Sara was reminded that there would be no going back to being friends with Jake. "Thank you, Nora. You look wonderful, too. I meant to ask you about your doctor's appointment. How did it go? Did you like the new doctor?"

"Humph! Dr. Richard Wellington is just a little too full of himself. I don't think I'll be going back after I get the results from my blood work."

"Oh, I'm sorry you didn't like him, Nora."

Meggie was brought outside just then, and she claimed the spotlight without even trying. Luke took her from John but wasn't allowed to keep her for long. Sara and Grandpa chuckled as Meggie reached out to first one and then another family member until she got to Gram. She was settling into this family life really quickly.

But when Gram sat down between Sara and Grandpa, still holding Meggie in her arms, Sara's fingers itched to take the baby and hold her once more. She barely noticed Nora's quick departure from her side.

"I think she's getting just a little tired," Gram said. The baby was looking around with almost a glazed look in her eyes. "Meggie, do you remember Sara?" Gram asked as she turned the baby toward Sara.

"Hi, Sweetness. Do you remember me?" Sara smiled at the baby.

Immediately, Meggie reached out to her. "Sawa."

Delighted that Meggie said her name, Sara wasn't sure if Meggie dove for her, or if she grabbed the baby. The next thing she knew, the baby was in her arms and had her head on Sara's shoulder.

"Oh, how sweet," Gram said. "She certainly does remember you, Sara."

Sara rocked the baby back and forth, loving the feel of her in her arms. She couldn't resist planting tiny kisses on her silky soft hair. Meggie was quickly claiming a piece of her heart.

"Well, would you look at that?" Grandpa asked moments later.

Gram smiled. "It seems as though Meggie was just waiting for your arms to fall asleep in, Sara."

Sara chuckled and tightened her hold on the baby. "I'll take that as a compliment."

"Oh, you should," Gram said. "I have to rock her for a long time before she goes to sleep. She'll fall right to sleep in Jake's arms, but not mine."

The bond Sara had felt that first day in Gram's kitchen grew even stronger as she sat and watched the party with Meggie in her arms. She knew she should lay the baby down, but she didn't want to let her go. Not yet.

୧ଈ

Jake was beginning to tire of trying to keep names and faces straight. He wanted to find Meggie and make sure she was all right. He wasn't used to letting others take care of her, and he'd made himself stand and make conversation for over an hour now. It was time to find his daughter.

He started across the yard, but seeing Meggie in Sara's arms once more stopped him in his tracks. Sara was rocking back and forth, staring down at the baby. From the looks of it, Meggie was sound asleep. Gram and Will were looking on and talking to her.

His first instinct was to do what he'd done that first day in Gram's kitchen. Just take her from Sara and make a quick run for it. But he couldn't do that. Not here. He wasn't about to make a scene in front of his family and friends.

An invisible link seemed to be forming between Sara and

his daughter, and he wasn't sure he liked it. Nor did he understand it. And he didn't have a clue what to do about it. He forced himself to walk casually up to the small group and smile. "She couldn't take any more attention, huh?"

Gram chuckled. "I guess not. She recognized Sara and reached out to her. It took her all of about a minute to crash."

"Doesn't take her long some nights. I guess I should be getting her home," Jake said, hoping his grandmother would agree, but knowing she wouldn't.

"It's early yet, Jake. We haven't even eaten yet. I'm sure Lydia will have a bed Meggie can sleep in for a while," Gram said. "Let me go ask." She was up and gone before Jake could stop her.

"Do you want to take her, Jake?" Sara asked softly.

Yes, he wanted to take her from Sara. There was something about the two of them so close together that pulled at his heart and created a longing within himself that he neither welcomed nor understood. But he was reminded of the look on Sara's face when he'd taken Meggie from her before, and he knew he wasn't going to let himself react that way again. The least he could do was let her hold his child for a few minutes.

"I don't want to jostle her too much. No need to wake her up," Jake said, although he was pretty sure nothing would wake Meggie up, as tired as she'd been lately.

Lydia came back outside with Gram. "I turned down the guest bed. I even have one of those bed rails to keep her from rolling off. She should be fine there. You know which room it is, Sara?"

Sara nodded and looked at Jake.

"Lead the way." He put his hand on her elbow to help her up from the bench she was sitting on and motioned for her to go first.

He followed Sara through the kitchen and up the stairs as she held his child in her arms. She turned to the right in the hall and they entered a small room with a twin bed that had indeed been turned down. A soft light lent a cozy glow to the scene.

Sara laid Meggie down, but the baby had a firm grip on her dress. She gently dislodged the little fingers, rolled the baby on her side, and rubbed her back. Meggie smiled in her sleep and plopped her thumb back into her mouth. Sara looked up at Jake and whispered, "Should I take her shoes off?"

Watching her with his child, Jake suddenly realized how very much Sara had lost and his heart twisted for her. He cleared his throat but still couldn't find his voice, so he just nodded.

He watched her fumble with one small shoe and then the other. Sara seemed to have forgotten he was there as she covered Meggie up with the sheet and caressed her cheek. "Sweet dreams, little Meggie."

She kissed her brow, stood, and backed away while he put the guardrail in place.

Jake bent over and kissed his daughter's cheek before turning back to Sara.

"Thank you, Jake." Her smile was real, but so was the sheen of tears in her eyes. Jake reached out and pulled her into his arms, wanting only to comfort her. Sara's head was on his shoulder, and they rocked back and forth for several minutes.

He wasn't sure what to say, he just wanted to make her feel better somehow. "Sara—"

Sara lifted her eyes to his and smiled through her tears. "Jake, I'm all right. Truly I am." Her voice broke for a moment before she continued. "It's just so good to hold a child."

Knowing he could never fully understand what Sara was feeling, Jake simply nodded, while he marveled that there was no bitterness in her eyes. "I'm sorry I took her away from you the other day."

Sara shook her head. "There's no need to apologize. I've seen you looking for her all evening. I think you're having a hard time trying to share her, and that's understandable. After all, it's just been the two of you since she was born."

That she read him so well came as no surprise to Jake. Sara had always understood him. But it was disconcerting that she still did after all these years.

His eyes strayed to her lips, and he found himself wondering if they tasted the same. Feeling the need to know, his head dipped and his lips lightly brushed hers. Sara responded. Her lips clung for a second, for two, before she pulled away.

Jake wanted to kiss her again, but his eyes met hers and he saw the confusion in them. What could he possibly be thinking? Sara was not in his future. She'd opted out of his past. Hadn't he learned anything over the years?

five

Sara's heart charged into triple time as she stood there looking at Jake. What just happened here? She'd wanted Jake to kiss her. Wanted him to hold her. The touch of his lips on hers felt familiar and comforting.

What was wrong with her? How could it feel so right to be in his arms? It'd been over between them long ago. She'd loved Wade. How could she be so disloyal to his memory?

The look in Jake's eyes mirrored her own confusion. She wanted both to reach out to him and to flee. She chose to run. "I'd better check on Grandpa," she said, backing out of the room.

Jake cleared his throat and nodded. He turned back to Meggie. Sara saw him bend down and kiss his daughter again before she turned and hurried back downstairs.

Sara didn't realize she was holding her breath until she entered the kitchen and saw that in reality, only a few minutes had passed since she and Jake had taken Meggie upstairs.

Ben was on his way out the door with more hamburger patties to put on the grill. Lydia was slicing onions and tomatoes. She'd commandeered Nora into tearing lettuce leaves and placing them on a big tray. Other family members were busy with the small jobs that always made huge gatherings somehow work. No one seemed to have missed them, or so Sara thought until she met her mother-in-law's chilly glance.

"There you are," Nora said. "I came in the house looking for you, and Lydia put me to work."

Sara hurried over and began helping Nora. "I'll do that for you."

Lydia chuckled. "I thought you came in to help out, Nora. If you'd asked, I could have told you Sara was upstairs putting the baby to bed."

The sound of Jake's heavy footsteps came down the stairs. When he entered the kitchen, Sara willed herself not to look at him, concentrating instead on tearing lettuce.

"Thanks for the loan of the room, Aunt Lydia," Jake said. "If you hear her wake up, please call me in."

"Of course, Jake. She'll be fine," Lydia reassured him. "You go on outside and enjoy your party. We'll listen for her."

"Thanks for getting her to sleep, Sara." Jake stood in the middle of the room, appearing to be waiting for her to say something.

Looking up and meeting his eyes, she said, "You're welcome. It was a pleasure to have her in my arms."

Jake gave a brief nod before heading outside, and Sara watched him go, remembering the feel of being in his arms just minutes ago. It'd felt like coming home, like—

"Sara, are you going to stand there staring into space, or help me with this lettuce?" Nora arched an eyebrow at her.

Sara ducked her head and continued tearing lettuce. She tried unsuccessfully to keep the color from stealing into her face. She'd been reliving Jake's kiss, and now the guilt that she'd enjoyed it washed over her. Wade had been gone over a year now, but it didn't seem right to be attracted to another man—especially when that man was his cousin. Yet right or wrong, she was drawn to Jake.

One glance at Nora told her that her mother-in-law wasn't happy about the short time Sara and Jake had spent together upstairs. The woman's lips were pursed together. Frown lines gathered between her eyebrows. Suddenly, Nora's hand pressed against her chest and she closed her eyes.

Sara reached out and touched Nora's shoulder. "Are you all right?"

Nora shook her head. "I'll be fine."

"You're sure? You look a little pale."

"I think I may be coming down with something. I do have a

headache and feel nauseous. I think I'll just get my purse and go on home."

"I'll go up and get your things, Nora," Lydia said, washing her hands at the sink.

"No, no! I can get them myself. I'll see myself out. You see to your guests." She hurried upstairs, leaving Lydia and Sara to stare at one another.

"I'm a little worried about her, Lydia. She hasn't seemed herself lately," Sara said.

"Maybe it's just stress. It's been a hard year for Nora," Lydia said. "I think I tend to forget that sometimes, she's just so. . .Nora." She shook her head. "I doubt I'd have been anywhere near as strong as she's been had I lost my only son."

"I think I'll go up and make sure she is all right," Sara said, wiping her hands. She ran lightly up the stairs and turned to the right to peek into Lydia's room where guests had been instructed to leave the items they didn't want to carry around all evening.

Nora wasn't in the bedroom. The bathroom door was ajar, and Sara could see she wasn't there, either. She came out of the room and glanced down the hall. Nora must have turned on the landing and gone out the front door. She'd call in a little while and make sure she made it home safely.

The door to the room Meggie was napping in was slightly ajar, and Sara quietly peeked inside. Surprise took her breath away. There, on her knees beside the bed, was Nora. Tears flooded Sara's eyes as she watched her mother-in-law reach out and gently smooth back the hair on Meggie's forehead. But when she saw Nora bend over to kiss the baby's cheek, Sara's hand quickly covered her mouth to quiet the sob that formed in her throat.

Knowing Nora thought she was alone, Sara quickly backed out of the room and tried to calm herself. She must have made some kind of noise, though, because Nora's head turned sharply and she swiftly got to her feet and joined Sara in the hall. Sara's first instinct was to give Nora a hug, but her mother-in-law had never been comfortable with genuine demonstrations of affection or comfort.

"You might ask Lydia if she has one of those gates to put up at the door so that the baby doesn't fall down the stairs," Nora said brusquely as she started down the hall.

"Yes, yes, I'll ask her," Sara answered.

"She could crawl to the end of bed and get down," Nora continued. "If she got out of the room she could get hurt."

On the landing leading to both the front and the back of the house, Nora stopped Sara from turning to go back to the kitchen. "Meggie is a beautiful child. But Jake only came home to find a mother for her," Nora whispered.

"Nora, we don't know that. He just wants Meggie to be raised around his family."

Nora shook her head and whispered more urgently, "Mark my words. He hurt you once before, he'll hurt you again. Only this time there'll be no Wade to pick up the pieces." She pulled her purse strap over her shoulder and took the flight of stairs leading to the front door, leaving Sara standing on the landing, speechless and feeling the weight of her loss all over again.

Nora didn't need to remind her that Wade was no longer here. She lived with that knowledge every day of her life, always wishing she hadn't wanted that ice cream. Oh, she knew that the wreck wasn't her fault. A drunk driver had plowed into Wade's car. Still, she'd been the one craving ice cream, and that was the only reason they were in the car at ten o'clock that night.

Nora had never implied that she was to blame. But in the back of her mind, Sara could never quiet the voice that kept telling her that if she hadn't wanted that ice cream so bad, Wade and her baby might still be here. *O Lord, please help me. I thought I was doing so well.*

"Sara? Nora?" Lydia called from the bottom of the stairs.

"It's me, Lydia." Sara brushed away the tears that'd fallen and hoped Lydia wouldn't be able to tell she'd been crying in the dim light. "Nora just left. She was checking on Meggie and told me to ask if you have one of those gates for the door."

"Oh my. I certainly do. I totally forgot about that." Lydia bustled up the stairs, passed Sara, and led the way to the storage closet at the end of the hall. By the time she'd pulled out the gate, Sara had herself under control.

They both peeked in at the sleeping child while making sure the gate was snug against the door frame.

"Look at that. A thumb sucker. If I remember right, Jake used to suck his thumb, too," Lydia whispered. They started back to the kitchen.

Downstairs, Lydia poured them both a glass of iced tea and led Sara out onto the deck where Ben was grilling burgers and wieners. She handed her a plate. "You eat and go enjoy yourself, Darlin'. Enjoy life a little."

Sara forced herself to fix a plate and eat. She managed to mingle with friends and family for the rest of the evening, taking care not to join any groups standing around Jake.

æ

Jake renewed acquaintances and re-bonded with family throughout the evening, all the while trying not to think of holding Sara in his arms and the kiss they had shared. Brief though it had been, it'd shaken him far more than he wanted to admit. He told himself he wasn't interested in starting up with Sara again, even if he could imagine that she might still care about him. All he wanted was to be able to raise Meggie in the same loving atmosphere he'd grown up in and make sure family was close by if anything should ever happen to him. That's all.

Yet when Sara came back outside with his aunt Lydia, Jake found his gaze seeking her out, in spite of the fact that he'd resolved to avoid her as much as possible. She'd looked so vulnerable putting Meggie down for her nap. And when he saw the tears in her eyes, he'd wanted to console her somehow. That's all. Just help her past that moment of sadness.

Now as their eyes met across the yard and Sara glanced away, he knew he'd only succeeded in making them both feel more uncomfortable with each other than they already had.

When he realized she was trying to avoid him by joining only the clusters of people he wasn't part of, he tried to make things easier by leaving whatever group she headed toward. It was a cat-and-mouse game in reverse. The last thing either of them seemed to want was to catch up with the other.

Jake wondered which of them was more relieved when the party started to break up.

ða

Sara had never been so glad for a party to end in her life. Trying to avoid Jake at his own welcome-home party had been draining enough, but once they were home, Grandpa wanted to rehash the whole evening over hot chocolate. Thankfully, he did most of the talking so all she had to do was add an agreeable murmur here and there.

"Nora left early, didn't she? I was a little surprised to see her there at all."

"She wasn't feeling well. I meant to call her to make sure she got home all right." Sara glanced at the clock and decided it was too late to call.

"More than likely, she just came for appearance's sake and left as soon as she could. We both know she isn't too happy about Jake coming back home." Grandpa leaned back in his chair and brought his cup to his mouth.

"I don't understand that, Grandpa. She used to ask about him and Melissa at every family gathering."

"That could have been more from curiosity than any kind of concern. Nora doesn't seem to care about many people these days. Just you. And I do worry that she's going to keep you from building a new life for yourself."

"I'm not going to let that happen. But she is Wade's mother, and I do feel a responsibility to her."

"I know you do." He drained his cup and took it to the sink to rinse out. He turned back to Sara. "You know, I think Nora needs to make a new life for herself. She's still a nice-looking woman. If she'd just soften up a bit, she could probably attract a man."

"That'd be wonderful, Grandpa, except I've heard her say she didn't want another man in her life too many times." Sara joined him at the sink and kissed him on the cheek. "But it's a great idea. We'll have to be on the lookout for someone."

The older man patted her on the back and nodded his head. "I'll talk to Ellie about it. If we put our heads together, we're bound to come up with someone."

Sara smiled to herself. *Looks like he's come up with one more reason to see Gram.* She really was going to have to watch those two a little closer from now on. "Let me know who you two come up with."

He crossed the room and started upstairs. "I'll do that, Darlin'. I sure will do that."

Sara straightened up the kitchen and headed up to her own room. It'd been a very long evening. She did hope her mother-in-law was all right. If Nora wasn't in church tomorrow morning, she'd check on her first thing when she got home from the service. Maybe Grandpa was right. A man in Nora's life might perk her up. She'd been a widow a long time.

Sara prepared for bed, still wondering about the tenderness she'd witnessed Nora showing Meggie at the party. She would have made a good grandmother. *And I would have made a good mother.* But neither was to be and she wasn't going to let herself slide into a self-pitying mode again. She'd spent quite enough time there.

There might come a day when she could think of starting a family with another man, but it wasn't now. Yet knowing that fact didn't keep thoughts of Jake at bay. Being in his arms for those few short moments had taken her back to a time when she'd felt completely at home there.

It was probably good that Nora had reminded her of how Wade had picked up the pieces. She'd been shattered the night of her birthday when Jake had accused her and Wade of seeing each other behind his back. He had walked up when Wade was giving her a casual kiss, assuring her that Jake would be there to wish her happy birthday soon. That was all it'd been, but Jake hadn't stayed around to hear an explanation. Instead, he'd flown into a rage and taken off.

She'd cried herself sick for weeks and even tried calling to talk to him. He was never in. Finally, Wade had gone up to college to talk to Jake. When he came back, it was with the news that Jake was getting married to someone else. Sara couldn't remember much of the rest of that year, except that Wade had always been there for her. He'd taken her wherever she needed to go, escorted her to all kinds of events, and helped her get over his cousin.

She'd come to love Wade in a whole different way than she'd loved Jake, and when he'd asked her to marry him, she hadn't hesitated. She'd said yes. There might not have been bells and whistles, but they'd had a comfortable relationship and a good marriage, and she missed him dearly.

Now she felt guilty, angry, and confused for being comforted by the very man who'd hurt her all those years ago.

ə̀

Jake tossed and turned all night. But it wasn't his old nightmare keeping him awake. He simply couldn't get Sara out of his mind. He threw off the covers and got out of bed. The sun was just coming up. He'd check on Meggie and go put the coffee on for Gram. It wasn't often anyone beat her up of a morning.

Meggie was already awake and playing with one of the stuffed animals in her bed. She looked up at him with that beautiful smile and reached out to him. "Dada!"

Nothing in this world felt as good as having his daughter in his arms. He changed her diaper and carried her downstairs to the playpen in the kitchen. After quickly putting the coffee on, he played hide-and-seek behind one of Meggie's big stuffed toys, while waiting for the coffee to brew. It'd just finished when Gram joined them.

"Well, this is a treat. Not often do I wake to the smell of coffee first thing in the morning." She crossed the room to give both Meggie and Jake a kiss on the cheek. "It's so nice to have you two here."

"I was hoping I'd beat you down." Jake kissed his grandmother on the cheek. "That's not easy to do."

Gram chuckled as she poured two cups of coffee and set his on the table. "I must have slept in this morning."

Jake sat down across from her and cradled the cup in both hands, savoring the rich aromatic smell before taking a sip.

"You haven't forgotten your promise, have you?"

"No, Gram, I haven't forgotten. I'll feed Meggie as soon as I get a cup of coffee in me and then go get her ready." It was Sunday, and he'd promised Gram that he and Meggie would go to Sunday school and church with her. As if he'd had a choice. Anyone who lived in Ellie Tanner's home went to church on Sunday.

He really didn't mind. Taking Meggie to church would be one less thing to feel guilty about, Jake realized as he prepared his daughter's oatmeal and juice, while Gram began working on their breakfast. He'd promised Melissa that if anything happened to her, he'd see to it that their child knew the Lord. And he wanted her to have a good relationship with God. Like he'd had before.

Watching Meggie try to feed herself took all of his attention. She did pretty well until he tried to help. Then she pulled back on the spoon, and oatmeal went flying. It kept him busy, just trying to keep everything from ending up on the floor.

Gram set a plate of bacon and eggs in front of him just as Meggie took her last bite.

"You eat your breakfast and I'll get Meggie dressed," Gram said, reaching to pick at his hair. "I think you'd better jump in the shower. Meggie got more oatmeal on you than on herself or the floor."

"Typical meal time with my daughter. Most of it ends up anywhere but inside her," Jake said, chuckling. He took Meggie from her high chair and handed her to Gram. "Thanks for your help, Gram. You'll know better what to dress her in than I would."

"You do fine, Jake. Meggie always looks adorable, don't

you, Sweetie? Let's see. Do we need to wash your hair this morning?" She chuckled and checked Meggie's hair. "No, looks like Daddy got all the mess today."

Jake joined her laughter and watched as she and his daughter left the room. He quickly ate his meal and rinsed off his plate before hurrying upstairs to get in the shower. You had to act fast with oatmeal. It acted like cement if it sat in one place too long.

❧

When Sara and her grandfather took their seats in church that morning, she knew something was up. A bevy of females was clustered in the middle of the aisle.

The last person she expected to see in church that Sunday was Jake Breland. But he was sitting beside Gram, looking very ill-at-ease with all the attention he and Meggie were getting. Meggie, however, seemed to be eating it all up as she sat in her daddy's lap. She looked adorable dressed in pink and white gingham. Luke came in late, took one look at the crowd around his brother, grinned, and then backtracked to enter the pew from the other side. Aunt Lydia, Uncle Ben, and John seated themselves in the pew behind them.

It appeared as if most of the young single women were busy welcoming Jake and his daughter home. If Nora was right in her assumption that he'd come home only to find a mother for Meggie, Sara figured he'd have several to choose from. For some reason that thought didn't set well with her, but she told herself it wasn't jealousy.

Too bad Nora wasn't here to see how many women seemed to be interested in exploring that very subject. Sara made a mental note to be sure to check on her as soon as she got home from church.

Finally, one of the deacons stood at the podium and cleared his throat, trying to get everyone's attention. Sara halfway expected to hear an announcement about an eligible bachelor being back in town. She was glad Jake had come to church, though. She hoped Gram was wrong in thinking that Jake's relationship with the Lord wasn't what it should be.

Sara tried to keep her mind on the service. She joined in the singing and heard Jake's baritone joining in. She'd forgotten what a beautiful voice he had. Meggie kept looking at her daddy's lips move, as if she'd never seen him sing before. She clapped when the first song was over, bringing chuckles from those around her.

More than once during the service, Sara had to force her attention away from Meggie and back to the sermon. The regular minister and his wife, David and Gina Morgan, were away on a missionary trip and were scheduled to return later in the week. Gina was one of Sara's best friends, and the couple had been a source of great strength for Sara over the past year. She really missed them. Gina's father, Tom Edwards, filled in for David, giving a good message on turning one's life over to God each and every day.

When the worship service came to an end, Sara hoped Grandpa wouldn't stand around talking for too long. She hurried out to the foyer ahead of him. Much as she wanted to reach out to Meggie, she didn't want to deal with Jake.

Looking back into the sanctuary, she recognized there was no need to worry about running into Jake. He and Meggie appeared to be held captive once more. Sara hadn't had any idea there were that many single women attending church, and she tried to tamp down the flash of jealousy she felt seeing Jake be the focus of all of their attention. Fortunately she didn't have to sort out her feelings, because just then she was approached by one of the deacons, who asked about the teddy bear project.

As soon as she and Gramps got home, Sara kicked off her heels and sat down to call Nora. But Nora didn't appear to be in the mood to talk. No, she wasn't sick. No, she didn't want company. Sara sighed as she hung up. She just wished Nora would move into town. Uncle Ben ran the ranch from his place. There was really no need for Nora to stay out there. It would make it so much easier for her to check on her from time to time.

Sara finished up the roast she'd put on before leaving for church that morning, but her thoughts kept returning to Meggie and how adorable she'd looked sitting in Jake's lap.

Grandpa said the prayer before the meal and then filled his plate. "What did you think of the reception Jake got at church this morning?"

Sara had been trying *not* to think of it. "Nora told me he'd only come home to find a mother for Meggie. If that's the case, it looks like he'll have his pick."

Grandpa chuckled. "Just 'cause he's got a lot to choose from, doesn't mean any of them would be his pick, Darlin'."

"Well, I'm sure it's none of my business." Sara passed the mashed potatoes to her grandfather.

"None of Nora's, that's for sure." He took a bite of roast and sighed appreciatively.

Sara's appetite had disappeared. She just pushed the food around on her plate. Why did it bother her so much to see all those women converging on Jake and Meggie this morning? She was going to have to get a grip on the situation. Jake was a handsome man, and he was bound to start dating sooner or later.

"This is really good, Sara," Grandpa said.

"Thank you." Sara smiled across the table at her grandfather. He was always so careful to compliment her on her cooking. Grandma had trained him well.

"What are you going to make for Sunday supper at Ellie's?"

Sara moaned inwardly. She didn't want to go to the supper at Gram's tonight. She wouldn't be able to avoid Jake, and she wasn't ready to deal with making small talk with him.

"I'm not sure I'm going tonight, Grandpa. I haven't spent much time with Deana lately, and I thought I'd see if she wanted to do something." Deana loved Gram's suppers, too. Sara hoped she could talk her into taking in a movie instead.

"And miss Sunday night supper?"

His face looked so crestfallen, Sara had to chuckle. "You can go, Grandpa. I'll make that blueberry pie you like so well for you to take."

"Well, all right, but I wish you'd change your mind and go. You love those suppers with the family."

And she did. But they weren't going to be the same now that Jake was back. It wouldn't be long before the whole family picked up on how uncomfortable they both felt around each other. Then everyone would start to feel uncomfortable too. Sara wanted to avoid that as long as possible.

Her heart tightened at the thought of spending less time with the family she loved. She didn't feel she could call Gram just to chat anymore, and now she wasn't sure she'd ever feel comfortable at Sunday supper again. With Jake's return, changes were occurring much faster than she'd anticipated. Part of her wished he'd stayed in Albuquerque, and the other part wanted nothing more than a repeat of last night. A repeat of that moment of feeling she was where she'd always been meant to be. Held securely in Jake Breland's arms.

six

With Meggie napping in her playpen close by, Jake sat at the kitchen table shelling pecans for Gram to make pies for her Sunday supper. He wondered how he'd forgotten about Gram's suppers. As a child and young man it'd been one of his favorite things about Sundays.

He'd probably blocked it out during his period of self-exile. He'd been so unhappy ten years ago. Crushed by Sara and Wade's betrayal, marrying Melissa and trying to make their marriage work despite the way it began—it had all been much easier to handle from Albuquerque.

For years, he'd avoided family gatherings, telling his grandmother they were going to Melissa's parents for all the holidays. They had spent some time with her family, but then her parents had been killed in an airplane crash. By that time, he was so used to not being in Sweet Springs, he had felt no desire to come home for the holidays. On those rare occasions when he'd made plans to come back, he had made sure word got out early. It seemed that Wade wasn't anxious to see him, either. He and Sara were either gone or busy with something else, and the result was that they'd never had to deal with seeing each other.

Now Jake sat at his grandmother's kitchen table, wondering if Sara and her grandfather would be there for supper and feeling disloyal to the mother of his child for even thinking about Sara. The familiar guilt that he'd never loved Melissa as much as she loved him washed over him. He'd tried. He had learned to love her, and he truly did miss her, but he'd always been suspicious about the way their marriage started. When Melissa came to him and told him she was pregnant, he did what he knew he should. He took responsibility for his

75

actions and asked her to marry him. And when she'd lost the baby a few weeks after their wedding, he'd kept his vows and promised Melissa they'd stay married and work to make it a good one, but in the back of his mind, there'd always been that question. Did Melissa trick him into marrying her? Had she ever been pregnant?

In spite of his suspicions, they had turned their marriage into a good one. Only Melissa had done most of the work that built their relationship, and Jake knew it. She'd been a good wife, and she would have been a wonderful mother to Meggie. He wished he could have loved her more. Now she was gone, and he could never go back and say the things she would have loved to hear from him.

Jake cracked another pecan, but his mind wasn't on what he was doing. He'd made so many mistakes. Oh, he'd tried to make things right. He'd taken responsibility for his actions and he'd asked the Lord for forgiveness. But he'd always felt he should do more to earn it, and now with Melissa gone, he never would be able to. All he could do was be the best father to Meggie that he could be. That he was determined to do. *Please, God. Let me do that right.*

"Tom had a good lesson today," Gram said, bringing him back to the present.

Jake nodded in agreement. "I didn't know Tom was the minister here."

"Oh, he's not. His son-in-law, David Morgan, is. He and Gina are due back from Guatemala this week some time."

"David Morgan? He's a preacher?" Jake remembered David Morgan from high school, but he'd never have thought his friend would become a minister.

Gram came over to the table and patted his shoulder. "He is. One of the best I've ever heard, too. I'm sorry, Jake. We really didn't keep you up to date very well, did we?"

"Well, Gram, it's not all your fault. I didn't show much interest in what went on in Sweet Springs." He reached up and patted the hand that rested on his shoulder. "I'm sorry."

"You're home now, though. You'll catch up in no time." She looked into the bowl of freshly shelled pecans. "That's probably enough for now."

"You sure? I haven't had a piece of your pecan pie in years. I could probably eat a whole one by myself." Jake grinned at her.

"No way, big brother," Luke said, coming in the back door.

Both Gram and Jake shushed him, and Luke took care that the door didn't slam behind him. He crossed the room to kiss his grandmother's cheek. "If you get a pie to yourself, so do I," he said to his brother.

"Help Jake shell a few more pecans, and I'll make an extra pie for you both to share."

The brothers grinned at each other and started working on the pecans. "Meggie sleeping?"

Jake nodded toward the playpen over in the corner and glanced at the clock. "She should be waking up any minute now."

"All that attention at church must have worn her out," Luke teased and then dodged the pecan Jake threw at him.

"I know it wore me out," Jake admitted. "I didn't know there were that many single women in all of Sweet Springs."

He had noticed that Sara hadn't approached him and Meggie. She seemed to be avoiding him, which he knew was for the best. Still, it rankled. He hadn't been able to sort through his feelings from the night before, and right this minute, he wasn't in a hurry to figure them out.

"I know what you mean," Luke said. "And I sure didn't know they were all so hard up they'd be fighting over my brother."

Even Gram joined in the laughter that time. "There were quite a few young women around our pew today."

"Well, if you'd like a clear field, Luke, you can get the word out that I'm not interested."

"Nah, you can let them down all by yourself, big brother."

"I didn't know we'd raised you two to think so highly of

yourselves." Gram stood facing the two men with her hands on her hips. "There were some fine young women in that group—some of whom might not want either of you, if they could hear the way you are talking right now."

"Aw, I'm just teasing Jake, Gram. You know how we are."

"Too bad some of those nice young ladies don't," she said, then shook her head and went back to her piecrusts, chuckling to herself every now and then.

⠦

Jake wasn't aware he was looking for Sara until Will showed up that night after church without her. He heard his grandmother ask Will why Sara hadn't come, but he couldn't quite make out the answer from across the room.

He didn't welcome the sharp pang of disappointment he felt. What was wrong with him? His mind warned him to stay as far away from Sara as possible, but the rest of him ignored the signals and looked for her at every opportunity.

"What's with you, Jake?" John joined him in a corner of the large wraparound porch. "You look like you've lost your best friend."

He had, Jake thought, a long time ago. For that's what he and Sara had started out as. Best friends. Both orphaned at early ages, they'd found they had much in common, and they'd formed a close friendship. There was nothing he hadn't been able to talk to her about, until the night he'd found her and Wade kissing. He shook his head. "No, I was just thinking back to when we were all young and how so much has changed."

"We had some great times, didn't we? This is a great family to be raised in. And Sweet Springs is a good town to grow up in. I can't imagine living anywhere else," John said. "I don't know how you stayed away as long as you did."

Jake shrugged. What could he say? That he was too immature to handle seeing Wade and Sara build a life together? He couldn't do that to Melissa's memory.

But he did have some questions he'd like answers to. "John,

why didn't you and Luke—anyone in the family for that matter—tell me Sara and Wade were seeing each other behind my back?"

Luke walked up just in time to hear the question and spoke up before John could say anything. "What are you talking about, Man? Sara was heartbroken when you married Melissa."

Jake shook his head. "No, she wasn't. She and Wade were seeing each other long before that."

"I think you're mistaken, Jake," Luke said.

"I saw them kissing!"

Luke and John looked at each other and shook their heads. "When was this?" John asked.

"On her birthday. I was late getting home. I'd had a flat tire."

Luke nodded. "I remember Sara was upset because you never showed up."

"But I did show up. And Wade and she were kissing."

Both Luke and John shook their heads. "I never even knew you were here," Luke said. "You went on back to school?"

"Yeah, I went back. I saw no reason to stay." Not then. But now, he knew he should have stayed to hear Sara out.

"Maybe Wade was just trying to comfort her."

Jake met John's eyes. "Yeah, right."

"Did you ask them about it?" John asked.

Jake turned away. He should have. But would that have changed anything? He shook his head. "From where I stood, there was no reason to ask. I saw them kissing."

"But you married Melissa just a couple of months after that." Luke looked closely at his brother. "We all thought you broke up with Sara because of Melissa."

"You thought wrong," Jake said. He wasn't going to tell them just why he'd married Melissa—there was no reason to now. But was it possible he'd been wrong about Wade and Sara? *Oh, dear Lord, could I have read everything wrong that night?*

"If there was anything going on between Sara and Wade before you married Melissa, we didn't know about it, Jake.

We'd have said something if we did," Luke insisted. "You know we would have."

More family and church members began to arrive, and the conversation came to a halt. But Jake did feel closer to his family than he had in years. Until he felt the anger fading away, he hadn't even realized he'd been holding a grudge, thinking they'd covered up for Wade and Sara. At least if Wade and Sara had been seeing each other, his family hadn't been trying to keep it from him.

He managed to enjoy the Sunday supper. The only glitch in the night was hearing so many people ask about Sara, especially when he had a feeling that he was the reason she was staying away.

❧

It'd taken some talking, but Deana did agree to go to the movies with Sara after church that night. Sara knew Deana was curious about why she was so determined not to go to Gram's, but Sara was given a reprieve from talking when, as they took their seats, the lights dimmed and the coming attractions started.

After the movie, they made their way out to the parking lot. "Well, the movie was okay, but I'm not sure it was worth missing one of Ellie's suppers. You going to tell me why we had to go tonight?" Deana asked as they walked to their cars.

Sara shrugged. "You never know how long a movie will be here."

"You know I'm not buying that answer, don't you? I think we need to talk."

Sara sighed. Deana knew her too well. "I'm not ready to talk about it yet."

Deana nodded. "Okay. You know where I am."

"Thanks, Deanie. For going with me tonight and for letting me off the hook."

"Oh, I'm just letting you off for the time being. Don't count on my forgetting."

"I know you won't." Sara chuckled as she got into her car.

but she knew she was in for a lengthy question-and-answer session one of these days.

She'd barely gotten the door unlocked when Grandpa pulled up. He'd brought her home a plate of sandwiches and various desserts, and she felt bad for not asking Deana over for coffee.

"Everyone asked about you, Sara. Said to tell you they missed you." He set the plate on the table.

"That's sweet. It's nice to know you're missed," Sara said, taking a seat at the table.

"Ellie said to tell you that she's taking no excuses next week. Said she expects you to be there."

Knowing Gram, she probably had already figured out why Sara hadn't made an appearance. Sara made a noncommittal sound before biting into a sandwich.

Grandpa poured himself a cup of coffee and sat down across from her while she ate.

"How was Meggie tonight?"

"The main attraction, of course. She laps up all that attention, but only to a point. Several of the women who were so attentive at church came to supper, but Meggie wouldn't have much to do with them. She's very selective about who she lets hold her." Grandpa laughed. "Linda Plunket tried to take her from Jake, and Meggie started crying. Jake had to take her upstairs to calm her down."

"Poor Linda. I'm sure that made her feel awkward."

"Ellie made her feel better by telling her that Meggie was just now getting used to the family holding her."

"She'll adjust to having new people around soon." Sara chuckled. "As a member of the Breland/Tanner family, she won't have much choice."

"They're a good bunch of people."

"Yes, they are." Sara bit into a chocolate brownie.

She loved the family she'd married into. She'd missed being there tonight. But the tension between her and Jake was so strong that everyone in the family would be picking up on it.

Nora had certainly not kept it a secret that she didn't like Jake being home. Any time spent in his company was bound to cause more tension between her and Nora.

Nora was right about one thing, Jake had hurt her in the past. She couldn't chance letting him hurt her again, and the easiest way to keep that from happening would be to see as little of Jake Breland as possible.

"You all right, Darlin'?" Grandpa nudged her hand.

"What? Oh, I'm fine, Grandpa." Or she would be—if she could just stop thinking about Jake.

ꙮ

Sara called Nora first thing the next morning, but it seemed she was feeling much better. So much so that she wanted Sara to meet her for lunch. Relieved that Nora wasn't feeling worse, Sara agreed.

Just as she hung up the phone, it rang again. "Sara dear," Gram said, "I missed you last night."

"I'm sorry, Gram. Deana and I went to the movies. Grandpa had a real good time, though."

Gram chuckled. "Your grandpa always manages to have a good time. Did he tell you that we're in cahoots together?"

"Oh?"

"We're trying to find a man we can introduce Nora to. Probably should be someone she's never met. You know, someone who hasn't been the victim of her sharp tongue?"

Sara couldn't contain her laughter. "Gram! You and Grandpa better watch yourselves. I don't think Nora will take kindly to you meddling in her life," she teased.

"Well, someone needs to. Maybe it'd stop her from meddling in everyone else's. Anyway, that's not what I called to talk to you about. It's time to start planning our annual family reunion, and I could use your help if it wouldn't be too much trouble."

Sara's newfound resolve to see less of the family melted. "Of course, I'll help you. What do you need me to do?"

"I thought maybe you could come over today, and we could map out a few things."

For once Sara was grateful for one of Nora's lunch dates. "Well, I am having lunch with Nora at noon."

"That will work out just fine. Meggie takes her nap around two o'clock. Would that work for you? Should give you plenty of time with Nora."

More time than she needed, actually. But she didn't want to run into Jake, either. She hesitated.

"Sara dear, Jake is going into the office this afternoon. You won't have to run into him."

Sara didn't know what to say. She didn't want to lie to Gram, but she knew the older woman would see through any excuse she could come up with. "I'll be there around two."

"Thank you, Dear. I knew I could count on you."

Sara hung up the phone with a half-smile on her face. Gram knew everything. Good thing one could trust her not to tell it all.

❧

This time Sara beat Nora to the diner. It was crowded when Sara got there, and Deana was busy in the back. Sara sighed with relief. One more reprieve from a heart to heart.

"Hello, Dear," Nora said, sliding into the booth opposite Sara. She picked up the menu and began to study it. "How was Sunday supper?"

"Grandpa said there was a good turnout. I didn't go." Her answer seemed to pique Nora's interest.

"Oh? Why not?"

Sara shrugged. She certainly wasn't going to tell Nora it was because Jake had held her in his arms and kissed her on Saturday night and she wasn't ready to try to look into his eyes and pretend it didn't happen. "Deana and I took in a movie."

Nora seemed pleased. "That's nice, Dear. I'm glad you are getting out more with friends like Deana."

Yes, of course she was, thought Sara. *As long as it wasn't a man—especially one named Jake Breland.* She immediately regretted her attitude.

"What are you doing this afternoon?" Nora asked as soon

as they'd given their order to the waitress.

"Gram called and asked if I'd help plan the family reunion."

When she saw Nora's face tighten up, her first instinct was to assure Nora that Jake wouldn't be there. Her second was to tell herself that she didn't have to explain her actions to Nora, and her third was to wonder if she'd imagined the tender scene between Nora and Meggie that she'd seen the other night. It certainly wasn't in evidence today.

"Is it that time again?" Nora frowned. "Seems like we just had a reunion."

"Actually, there wasn't one last year. There was too much grieving. But Gram doesn't want her family losing touch, and I'm glad she's going ahead with this one. I love the Breland/Tanner reunions."

"Well, I'd think she'd have enough help with Jake home. He could help her plan."

"Nora, you know men don't really like to plan these kinds of things." Sara was relieved that their lunch was served just then. Her mother-in-law's tone was turning chillier by the minute. Sara sighed and wished she'd just kept quiet about helping Gram. But Nora wouldn't like it if she thought she was being kept in the dark. Sara was going to have to keep these lunches with Nora to a minimum. All she seemed to get out of them lately was a bad case of indigestion.

❧

"Come in, Dear. Thank you so much for offering to help me with this." Gram met her at the door and led the way to the kitchen, where she checked on the contents of a large pot simmering on the back of the stove. She poured two cups of coffee and brought them to the table, where a plate of chocolate chip cookies rested. "I put a roast on before Jake left for the office, Meggie just went down for her nap, so we should have several hours of uninterrupted time."

"Looks like you have everything under control, Gram. How are you doing? Remember my offer to help with Meggie if this all gets too much for you." She took a sip of coffee and watched the older woman gather tablets and pencils before joining her at the table.

"I do remember, and I'll keep it in mind," Gram said, sitting down. "Right now, with Jake here of a morning, and Meggie sleeping in the afternoon, it's working out pretty well."

She certainly looked none the worse for wear, but she always had seemed to have the energy of a woman half her age. Sara could only hope that she aged as well.

Gram pulled out the list of family members and handed it to Sara. "I'm really hoping Laci will be able to come home for this reunion. I haven't seen that child in two years, but she's promised to try."

Laci was John's sister, and she'd moved to Dallas several years back to study design. Now she owned her own interior design company. Starting a new business had kept her extra busy, and she hadn't been able to make it home in quite some time.

"What date are you targeting? It's the end of May now."

Ellie nodded her head and looked at the calendar. "I know I'm cutting it close, but I'd like to try for the Fourth of July. A lot of family may have already made plans, but I'd dearly love to have as much of my family together as I can this Independence Day."

"Well, let's go for it. What do you want me to do?"

"Sara, I don't know what I'd do without you. I guess the first thing is to call my sister and brother in Arkansas and see if they can come. Then, there's Bill's brother and family. . . ."

The next few hours flew by as they kept the phone busy. Almost everyone was as anxious to pick up with the family reunion as Gram was. She had plenty of room in her home, but there was no way she could put everyone up. Sara called both motels in town for information about reserving rooms. She'd just poured them both a fresh cup of coffee when the back door opened.

Luke entered and gave both his grandmother and Sara a kiss on the cheek. He turned to his grandmother with a wide grin. "It sure smells good in here. Think you could set a plate for one more?"

Gram grinned up at him. "Since when do you have to ask?"

Realizing that Jake would be coming in soon, Sara quickly gathered her things together and crossed the room to kiss the older woman on the cheek. "I didn't realize it was getting so late. I'd better check on Grandpa. You call me if you think of anything else you need me to do, okay?"

"I will, Dear. Thank you for helping today."

"You're welcome," Sara said as she headed for the door.

"Hey, where's my kiss?" Luke asked.

Sara shook her head and turned to kiss him on the cheek. "Night, Luke."

He reached out and tousled her hair. "Night, Sara."

She pulled the door shut behind her and sighed with relief that she'd been able to leave without running into Jake again. If only she could feel as comfortable around him as she felt around Luke.

seven

After several days had passed without running into Jake, Sara began to relax. Since Gram had told her that Jake went to the office each afternoon, Sara timed her visits with the older woman when she was sure that he wouldn't be there.

Plans for the reunion were moving along. They'd contacted Laci, and she'd promised she'd try her best to come. A couple of Gram's great-nieces and nephews had let her know they were coming as well. Sara loved hearing the excitement in Gram's voice and was glad things were coming together so well.

Nora hadn't expressed much excitement about the reunion, but she didn't get excited about too much these days. Sara was beginning to think Grandpa and Gram were right: Maybe Nora did need a man in her life.

Sara had just finished making calls to remind the ladies of the church about the next teddy bear-making meeting and poured herself a glass of iced tea, when the phone rang.

"Hi, Sara," the voice on the other end said after Sara had answered the phone. "I hear you've been quite busy since we've been gone."

"Gina! You're back. When did you get in? Did you have a good trip? When can we get together?"

"We got in last night, the trip was really rewarding, and anytime is good for me. I missed you!"

"How about the diner?" Sara looked at the clock. The lunch crowd would have cleared out by now. "In about thirty minutes?"

"I'll be there. I can't wait to get caught up on what's been happening in Sweet Springs."

A short while later, Sara parked at the diner. Gina was

already waiting in a booth but got to her feet as soon as she spotted Sara. The two friends hugged and grinned at each other before taking their seats.

"A month is just too long for you and David to be gone. I really have missed you."

"We're glad to be home. But the trip really was such an eye-opener for me. We take so many things for granted here, Sara. The orphanage is growing so fast, I'm just glad we've been able to help down there. The children will steal your heart."

"I'm glad you were able to do it. Tom did a real good job while y'all were gone."

"I'll tell him you said so. He and Mom are going down to Guatemala with the next work group."

The waitress came for their order, and they both settled for apple pie and coffee. As soon as they were left alone, Gina grinned over at Sara.

"I hear we have a couple of new faces in town—and that they caused quite a stir in church on Sunday."

Sara chuckled and nodded. "Jake and Meggie. He's going into practice with John. They're staying at Gram's for now."

"That's what I understood." Gina turned serious. "How is he doing as a single parent?"

"He's very good with Meggie. And she's adorable, Gina. I know exactly what you mean by stealing your heart. She stole mine the very first day."

"It hasn't been too hard on you, seeing her. . ."

Sara shook her head. "The first day at Gram's, she reached out to me, and it was as if God gave me what I needed, a child to hold, even if only for a few minutes. It was time."

Deana came out from the kitchen, bringing their pie and coffee, and joined them for a few minutes before the coffee-break crowd descended upon the diner. "What was time?" she asked Sara.

"For me to hold a baby."

"Ah, Meggie, right? Jake brought her in with him the other day, and she really is a cutie. It won't be long before she's walking. I hope she's not too much for Ellie then."

"So do I. Jake is only working part of the day now, but that can't last forever."

The bell above the door tinkled, and the three of them looked toward the door.

Deana grinned. In came David, Jake, and John. "Do you think they have radar and know when we're talking about them?"

She stood up and stretched. "The afternoon crowd arrives. It's back to the grindstone for me. One of these days, I'd like to sit down and have a real gab session."

"We'll have to get together soon and have a real hen party," Gina said.

Deana nodded on her way back to the kitchen. "Sounds good to me. Let me know when."

David slid in beside his wife and kissed her on the cheek, while John pulled a chair to the end of the table, leaving the space beside Sara for Jake.

Sara scooted over to give him more room, knowing she'd congratulated herself too soon for managing not to run into him. From Jake's quick shrug and half smile, she surmised he hadn't expected to run into her, either. She hoped the flurry of greetings everyone else was involved in would help keep them from noticing how uncomfortable she and Jake were.

"I thought you were catching up in the church office this afternoon," Gina quizzed her husband.

"He was," John said. "But word had it that you two were back, and Jake and I searched him out and convinced him to take a break with us."

"Jake, it's good to see you again." Gina smiled across the table at him. "But I'm really looking forward to meeting your daughter. I've heard she's really something."

Sara watched Jake's smile turn into a proud-papa grin.

"She is that. You come by anytime. I'm always happy to show her off."

"Oh, we'll be there for Sunday supper, if not before," David said. "Ellie is one of our favorite people."

"How's she making out, keeping up with Meggie?" Gina asked.

"So far, so good. But I'm hoping it won't be for too long. I know Gram isn't getting any younger. I've been in contact with a realtor, and I'm going to look at a few places this weekend. But what I'm really going to need is a housekeeper to watch over Meggie for me. Any ideas on how to find one?"

"Have you tried the employment office?"

"Not yet. I was hoping to find someone through recommendations from people I know and trust."

"Let me think on it," David said. "Maybe I can come up with someone."

"In the meantime, if Ellie needs help, feel free to call," Gina offered.

Jake glanced at Sara and back to Gina. "Thanks. A lot of people are willing to help Gram, and John is letting me take my time getting settled."

"There's no hurry," John interjected. "I'm just thankful you've agreed to come in as a partner." He looked over at David and Gina. "Now, we want to know all about your trip. How is Guatemala?"

David and Gina didn't need any more coaxing to talk about their experiences in Guatemala. Sara tried to listen intently as they explained the ongoing work at the orphanage, but part of her was attuned to each and every breath Jake took. She was relieved when the impromptu gathering came to an end.

&

Jake had enjoyed the afternoon. He liked getting to know David and Gina all over again. From all he'd heard, David made a wonderful minister. He found himself looking forward to hearing him on Sunday.

The only rough spot in the afternoon had been when they'd first entered the diner and he'd found himself sitting next to Sara. He felt like a fumbling teenager as he drank coffee and ate his pie, trying very hard not to let her know how totally aware of her he was. Obviously they were going to be running into each other more often. They had family and friends in common, and Sweet Springs was not a large city where he could lose himself in the crowds. Hopefully he and Sara would soon get used to being around each other. He was back to stay, and he certainly couldn't see Sara moving away.

When Jake got back to the office, a message from Gram was waiting for him, and he quickly punched in the number. She answered on the fifth ring.

"Gram, is anything wrong?"

"I don't think it's serious, but Meggie's been a little fussy this afternoon. She doesn't have a fever, but I can't get her to eat a thing and she's been crying off and on. Do you think she might be cutting a new tooth?"

"Probably her first molar. I'll stop on the way home and get some of that stuff that numbs her gums. Maybe that will help."

"That's what I was going to ask you to do. Poor baby."

Jake could hear Meggie crying and Gram making soothing noises to her. "I'll be home as soon as I get it, Gram."

Jake hurried down the street to the drugstore. It hadn't changed much from when he was young. It was probably one of the few drugstores left that still boasted a real soda bar. Jake grinned, remembering all the fun he'd had here as a kid. It was nice to know that some things stayed the same. He'd have to bring Meggie in for a soda when she got a little older.

"Jake?" a soft voice inquired. "Is Meggie sick?"

He turned to see the concerned look in Sara's eyes. "Not sick, really. We think she's teething."

"Oh, that's good. Well, not good for Meggie, but I'm glad it's nothing more serious."

"Thank you, Sara." He motioned to the shelf in front of him. "I think one of these will help."

Sara nodded. "I'm sure it will."

"If I can only figure out which one to buy." He pulled two different brands off the shelf and turned to her. "Do you have any idea which one I should go with?"

Sara looked at both and shrugged. "I think either one will be all right. I'm sorry, Jake. I really don't know which brand to go with."

"Don't feel bad, Sara. Neither do I, and I've bought it before." He put one back on the shelf and turned to her again. He wanted to say more but didn't know what to say. "I guess I'd better get it home."

"Yes. I hope it works quickly. Give Meggie a hug for me?"

Jake nodded. "I will." He hurried to the checkout counter. It seemed to be the day for running into Sara. Maybe with time, it'd get easier. But somehow he knew that wasn't gong to happen until they'd confronted the past, and he wasn't looking forward to that conversation at all. Not one bit.

★

Sara had left the diner with the beginning of a headache and had stopped at the drugstore to pick up some aspirin. She left with a full-blown headache and started home wondering when and where she was going to run into Jake again.

She'd certainly made up for lost time today. She would have to try harder if she was going to manage to miss running into him at every turn. Was it even possible to avoid him? And was running into him, being in close proximity to him, ever going to get any easier?

That evening while fixing supper, Sara told Grandpa about David and Gina's trip as well as about running into Jake at the drugstore and learning of Meggie's teething difficulties. When they sat down to eat, he thanked the Lord for bringing David and Gina home safely and asked that Meggie feel better real soon.

Sara couldn't help but smile. She knew Grandpa was as taken with Meggie as she was.

All through supper, she told herself not to worry about the little girl, but she kept wondering if the problem involved more than teething. Could she have a cold or maybe a childhood disease?

After she'd cleaned the kitchen, Sara could stand it no longer. It didn't matter who answered the phone. She had to know how Meggie was. She picked up the phone and dialed Gram's number.

"Hello?" Gram answered.

"Gram? How is Meggie? I saw Jake in the drugstore—"

"She's fine now. That teething medicine worked like a charm. We even managed to get some supper down her. Jake's giving her a bath now. We think she'll be okay."

"Oh, good. I just wanted to make sure it was nothing more serious." Sara pictured Jake bathing Meggie and putting her to sleep. He really was a wonderful daddy.

"No, we're sure she's teething. Her little gum is real swollen. We'll doctor her good before she goes to sleep. Hopefully that tooth will come right on through."

"I'll pray it does. If you need anything, you call, okay?"

"I will, Sara. Thank you for checking."

Sara sighed with relief as she hung up the phone. Life was complicated enough without Meggie getting sick.

20

That Sunday morning, Jake listened closely to David's sermon. At first he listened mostly from curiosity about how someone he had known back in high school would preach. But soon the content of the sermon gripped his attention. It was on forgiveness—how we should forgive others as Jesus forgives us and forgive ourselves once we've been forgiven. David went on to describe the importance of going forward rather than dwelling in the past.

Jake wanted to move forward with his life. He was tired of living in the past. He wanted a better relationship with the Lord. He left church feeling for the first time as if maybe that would be possible. If Sara was at Gram's supper that night, he was going to talk to her. It was time to mend the past.

20

Sara knew she couldn't get out of going to Gram's Sunday supper, and she really didn't want to. It was a sort of welcome home for David and Gina, and she would never hurt them by staying away. She spent the afternoon baking a cake and making a platter of sandwiches to take. Wanting to help Gram as much as she could, she and Will took separate cars to church that evening so she could hurry over as soon as services were over.

Thankfully, others had already arrived when she got there, so Sara went straight to the kitchen to help Gram get things on the table. The turnout was large, as she knew it would be. Everyone wanted to welcome David and Gina home. Sara was hopeful that she and Jake could mingle without running into each other.

Somehow they managed to do just that. Or at least she did. By keeping a careful eye on which direction Jake was headed, she was able to move from one room to another just a step before or behind him.

She helped Gram keep the table full, took a turn washing up dishes, and still managed to visit. She even got to hold Meggie for a minute before Lydia claimed the little girl. All in all things were going better than she'd expected. Even Nora seemed to relax and enjoy herself.

Sara was headed back around the living room to pick up empty plates and cups when someone tapped her on the back. She turned to find Jake smiling down at her.

"Sara, can we talk?"

"Now? Here?" Sara hated sounding so breathless.

Jake looked around. "How about out on the porch?"

"All right," she said, doubt coloring her voice. She and Jake had been trying to stay out of each other's way ever since he came home. Now he wanted to talk?

Jake steered her to the side door, and when they got outside, he led her to a quiet corner. "I don't quite know how to go about this," he said, running his fingers through his hair. "But Gram says it's time."

"Time for what, Jake?"

"To try to call a truce or something so that we can co-exist in this town without making everyone around us uncomfortable. And today, David's sermon was on forgiveness. I just—"

"Jake, is that what this is all about?" Sara smiled up at him. "Because if it is, I forgave you for dumping me, long ago."

Jake's dark eyes glittered in the dark. "Dumping you? You were the one who was seeing my cousin behind my back."

"What are you talking about, Jake?" Sara whispered hoarsely. "I wasn't seeing Wade behind your back."

"Well, tell me who it was you were kissing that night. It certainly looked like Wade."

Sara gasped and turned around. She headed down the steps and ran out to her car, but Jake caught up with her before she got the door open.

"Sara, answer me." Jake's hand kept her from opening the car door.

"You lost the right to ask that question when you turned and walked away without listening to me that night." Sara looked back at the house and was relieved that no one seemed to have noticed them.

"Then it wasn't you I saw kissing Wade that night?"

"There was nothing going on between us, Jake. Nothing."

"That's not the way it looked to me. Not after I'd received several anonymous notes telling me different, that very week. And especially not after I saw you in Wade's arms."

"What are you talking about? I don't know anything about any notes. And Wade was just comforting me when I got upset because you hadn't shown up."

"Yeah, right."

"I don't owe you any explanations, Jake. You wouldn't listen that night. It wouldn't make any difference now. But I did *not* cheat on you. Wade and I didn't even start dating until after you married Melissa. From where I stand, it looks like you were the one doing the cheating."

Jake turned Sara to face him. "I never dated Melissa until after I saw you and Wade kissing that night."

"But you married her just a few months later."

"Yes, I did. But I wasn't seeing her before that night." Jake couldn't bring himself to tell Sara the full story—that after he had returned to college he had gotten drunk for the first and only time in his life and that weeks later Melissa had told him that she was pregnant with his child from that night.

"Wade said you admitted dating her when he went up to college to tell you there was nothing going on between us."

"Then he lied to you. And he never told me there was nothing going on between you two. He said that you didn't want to hurt me, but that you and he were in love. That he'd been in love with you for years."

"No! Wade wouldn't lie to me. He went to talk to you because I was so upset and I could never get you on the phone. He said he'd straighten everything out. Then when he came home, he said you were getting married."

"That much was true," Jake admitted. "I was getting married." He could never betray his dead wife by telling Sara that he got engaged because of Melissa's pregnancy. Besides, it would probably seem like a lame excuse. No one else knew of the pregnancy; Melissa had lost the child shortly after their wedding. He shook his head. Nothing he could do or say was going to change the past. The only thing he and Sara had was the future.

"Sara. Please. Can we call a truce? Can we put the past to rest and start over?"

"You're telling me my husband lied to me. How can you expect me to just put that to rest, Jake? I don't know that I can." Sara pulled on the door to the car, and Jake moved his hand away.

"I'm sorry, Sara."

"So am I, Jake." She got in the car, started the engine, and pulled away.

Jake watched her leave, feeling a mixture of regret and relief. Regret that he'd brought her more pain, but relief that the past was finally in the open. His heart felt lighter in the knowledge that while his cousin had betrayed him, Sara hadn't—at least not knowingly. But that relief ended when he realized that while Sara was innocent, he and Wade had chosen to act in ways that damaged many lives. And the pain from those actions lived on.

eight

All Sara wanted to do was keep driving—east to Roswell, west to Las Cruces—anywhere away from Sweet Springs. But she knew Grandpa would worry if he came home and she wasn't there. He'd be worried enough already that she hadn't told him she was leaving Gram's.

So she drove home the long way, up and down one tree-lined street after another, until she thought she had herself under control. Then she went home and dialed Gram's number.

Thankfully, Luke answered the phone. It was easy to convince him she wasn't feeling well without raising too many questions. He promised to tell Gramps she went home early and told her he hoped she felt better real soon.

Sara hoped so too, but somehow she doubted it. Jake had just told her that Wade had lied about them. How could she accept that her whole married life had been based on a lie? *Dear Lord, how could that be?* Wade had been a good husband, faithful and loving. He wouldn't have lied to her, would he?

She shook her head. No. He wouldn't. And it didn't matter, anyway. Wade wasn't here to defend himself, and she wasn't going to start doubting him now.

She put the water on to make some hot tea and paced the kitchen while she waited for the kettle to whistle.

No matter how hard she tried to suppress them, questions about the past kept surfacing. How could Jake have thought she was seeing Wade back then? She'd been crazy about Jake from their very first date. That was what had hurt so much. He hadn't trusted her. It'd taken so long for her to get over him. Wade had been there, that was true, but it didn't mean he'd been in love with her all that time or that he'd been trying to break her and Jake up.

98

No, Jake was mistaken. Or making excuses for his actions that night. Wade was her husband, and she knew him.

The kettle whistled and Sara quickly made a cup of tea and took it up to her room, but the drink sat untouched as she sat in the rocker by the window and looked out. How could she and Jake possibly bury the past when a whole new set of questions had just been raised?

&

Jake shook his head as he watched the taillights of Sara's car disappear. If he could manage to physically kick himself, he would. As it stood, he was seriously thinking of getting his brother to do it for him. Luke would oblige, but he would have questions Jake wasn't ready to answer. It seemed he'd made more of a mess of things than they were before he'd started.

He slowly walked back into the house and went up to check on his sleeping daughter. He'd just put Meggie to bed when he'd come back downstairs earlier and spotted Sara in the dining room. He'd been looking for a chance to talk to her all night, but she seemed to be in any room except the one he was in. So he'd quickly grabbed the chance presented to him and sought to clear the air between them. Oh, yeah, he'd cleared things up all right.

Fat chance of any truce being called now. He should have just asked that they start over, instead of actually going into the past with Sara. Now it looked like he was trying to excuse his actions by blaming a man who was no longer around to defend himself.

And wasn't that exactly what he had done? He was the one who hadn't given Sara a chance to explain anything that night. He was the one who'd gotten drunk and couldn't even remember what he'd done that night. All he knew was what Melissa had told him, and that had resulted in their marriage.

Oh, Wade may have used everything to his advantage, but it was Jake who'd given him that chance by not trusting Sara in the first place. Even if Wade had told him the truth, Jake knew the outcome wouldn't have changed. By then it was too late. Melissa had told him that she was pregnant.

Jake felt sickened by his behavior. He'd blamed everyone around him for his own mistakes. Oh, he thought he'd accepted responsibility for his actions by marrying Melissa. But he'd continued to blame Wade and Sara for his reactions to seeing them together that night.

He looked down on his daughter as she slept peacefully and marveled that the Lord had allowed him to be her father. To Meggie, he was just "dada," and she loved him unconditionally. Of course she didn't know what a mess he'd made of so many things. Jake hoped she'd never have to know.

He wished he could just stay upstairs by himself. But plenty of people were still visiting, and Gram could probably use his help. He bent down and kissed Meggie's softly scented cheek before heading back downstairs.

David looked up from refilling his coffee cup when Jake entered the dining room. "Been checking on Meggie?" he asked.

Jake nodded and chuckled. "She's sleeping soundly, thank goodness. She's been teething this week, and she's still not used to having quite so many people around."

"Changes can be tiring for a baby," David agreed. He took a sip of coffee. "I saw you walk Sara to her car a little while ago. Was she not feeling well?"

Surprised by the quick change of subject, Jake looked around and was relieved that they had the room to themselves. "I think she was fine before she talked to me. Sara and I have been finding it a little difficult, being part of the same family."

David nodded. "I noticed the two of you seemed a little uncomfortable the other day at Deana's. Anything you want to talk about?"

Jake saw only genuine concern in David's eyes. But he shook his head and nodded toward the doorway, where Gina and Lydia were entering. "Thanks for the offer. Maybe one of these days. Now's not a good time."

"Just so you know, I always have the time."

Jake smiled and nodded. "I'll remember that."

He greeted the two women and went through to the kitchen to see if Gram needed anything. It was the least he could do after running off her best helper.

≈

Funny how when you didn't want to run into a person, you couldn't seem to miss them, but when you wanted to run into someone, they were nowhere to be found, Jake thought. He'd been to Deana's at lunchtime two days in a row. He'd made several grocery runs for Gram and even strolled Meggie to the ice cream parlor last night, but Sara was nowhere to be found. He'd even checked out the drugstore to no avail. He was beginning to wonder if she'd left the country.

His search for a house wasn't turning up anything, either. He wanted an older home in town, in good condition. So, it seemed, did everyone who owned one. The ones that were available were either too little or too big.

Several lots were for sale, however, and after an initial meeting with a local architect and builder, it looked like he'd be at Gram's until he could have plans drawn up and a home built. Now, if he could just convince her to let him hire a housekeeper to help her out.

He approached the subject again at supper, when he had Luke to support his efforts. "Gram, I think it's time we put an ad in the paper to see if we can find a housekeeper to help you out."

Gram looked up at him, her knife poised motionless above a half-buttered biscuit. "Jake, I told you, I don't want some strange woman taking care of my house or helping me with my great-grandchild."

"But I know Meggie is a handful." Jake cut the chicken-fried steak into bite-sized pieces for his daughter and handed her a child-sized fork. She loved spearing food and feeding herself. He looked back at his grandmother and continued, "She's going to be walking and climbing before long. I don't want her wearing you out."

"Jake's right," Luke chimed in. "Meggie will run you ragged in no time once she starts walking. You are going to need some help."

"Lydia has been coming over some."

Jake nodded. "Uh-huh, and John said she told him that you practically run her off every time she mentions helping out."

"She has a house of her own to run and a husband to take care of."

Jake spooned some mashed potatoes onto Meggie's plate, and she gave him a cheesy grin.

"Anyone want more tea?" Gram started to get up.

"You sit, Gram." Luke got up and brought the pitcher over to the table. "Jake and I can certainly wait on ourselves."

"You'd think I was an old invalid, the way you two talk," she grumbled, lifting her glass for a refill.

"No, we don't," Jake answered, "and I certainly don't want our being here to turn you into one. How about this?" he added as he handed Meggie her sippy cup. "Do you think there might be a teenager or two from church who would want a part-time job? One who could come in afternoons and on Saturdays to help out?"

Gram looked over at him and smiled. "Now that I might be willing to think about. It just might work. I think there are one or two who could use the money."

Jake breathed a sigh of relief, and he and Luke did a high-five. Their grandmother could be one stubborn lady.

≈

Sara had been trying to keep busy. She'd helped Grandpa in the garden, she'd made ten more teddy bears, and she'd rearranged the living room. She'd stayed away from Deana's, the grocery store, and downtown in general.

But while she'd successfully avoided Jake, she hadn't been able to put him and what he'd said out of her mind. She kept going over the conversation with him. What bothered her the most was her reaction to the knowledge that Jake hadn't been seeing Melissa all along like she'd thought. He truly did seem to think that she and Wade had been seeing each other, and if that was true, then he had cared about her. Even though it shouldn't matter after all these years, she wanted to believe that Jake had loved her. And that's what troubled her most of all—the realization that she still felt something for Jake.

Recognizing that she had to talk to someone who might give her some insight into the past, she invited Gina and David to supper. Grandpa and David were out inspecting the garden before starting a game of horseshoes. Gina insisted on helping Sara do most of the dishes before they served dessert.

"Okay, my friend. Open up," Gina said, as she helped clear the table. "I know something is bothering you."

"You're right about that." Sara smiled at her friend. "What gave me away? The panic in my voice as I issued my last-minute invitation?"

Gina chuckled and shook her head. "No, I think it was last week at Deana's. The tension between you and Jake."

Sara sank her hands into the hot water and started washing a plate. "So much for thinking no one could tell."

Gina gave her a quick hug and took the plate from her. "I take it it's not been easy to adjust to him being back?"

"Loving his family so much doesn't make it any easier. They all mean so much to me, I don't want to have to give them up."

"As if they'd let you! Jake hasn't told you to stay away or anything like that, surely—"

"No." Sara shook her head. "In fact, he'd like us to call a truce. To get past our past, so to speak."

"Well, that's one way to put it. Can you do that?"

"Oh, Gina, I want to. I really do. Obviously we're making it hard on everyone around us. We have the same family and friends. It's not fair to you all."

"But?"

"But Jake told me something the other night that I find hard to believe."

"What was that?"

"Remember when Wade went up to college to talk to Jake? And he came back and said Jake was getting married?"

Gina leaned against the counter and nodded. "I remember."

Sara scrubbed another plate. "Jake says that Wade told him that we—Wade and I—were in love."

"Ah. . ."

"Jake said that Wade had been in love with me for a long time before that."

"Does that surprise you? Surely you knew that."

Sara closed her eyes and shook her head. "No, I didn't. I thought he was just my good friend."

"Oh. . ." Gina took the plate from Sara and dried it. Then she turned Sara around and led her back to the table. "And now you're wondering if Jake is telling the truth about what Wade said to him?"

Sara nodded. "I never knew Wade to lie to me."

"Did he ever tell you he didn't love you while you were dating Jake?"

"Well, no. He knew I was crazy about Jake. But if he told Jake that we were in love with each other, he lied to Jake."

Gina nodded. "That's true." She rubbed Sara's tense shoulders. "Sara honey, I don't know what to tell you. I can tell you that I always had the impression Wade was in love with you. Not that he was actively trying to break you and Jake up, but that he'd be there in the wings if you ever needed him."

"Why didn't I see that?"

"All you could see back then was Jake."

"Well, I'm not sure the same could be said about Jake. He said he didn't start seeing Melissa until he found Wade kissing me that night. But that's pretty hard to believe."

Gina shook her head and went back to the sink. This time she washed. "Not to me."

Sara took the plate she handed her and began to dry. "Why not?"

"Because I saw the way he looked at you, Sara. I think Jake was crazy about you."

Sara shook her head and continued drying dishes, mulling over what Gina had said.

"I'll never know for sure, will I?"

"I don't know, Sara. But I do know one thing from experience. None of us can redo what's in the past. All we can do is go forward."

Sara took the dishcloth from Gina and wiped down the counter. "I know you're right. It's just not easy."

"No, it's not." Gina drained the dishwater and turned to Sara. "You haven't asked for my advice, but I'm going to give it anyway."

"You know I always value your opinion."

"I'd say put the past to rest, call a truce with Jake, and go forward. Wherever that takes you."

Before Sara could answer, the screen door opened and Grandpa stuck his head in. "Sure is nice out here. You girls going to join us?"

"We'll be right there, Grandpa."

☙

Jake watched his daughter staring at the room full of other children. Meggie didn't seem to be sure she wanted to stay with the other toddlers. The woman who cared for them on Wednesday evenings at church showed Meggie a toy and introduced her to another little girl. Jake stayed until his daughter seemed to relax and become curious about the other children. He started to ease out the door and felt his heartstrings tug when Meggie casually waved her little hand and said, "Bye, Dada." Pride in the fact that she was handling his departure so well warred with the ache in his heart from realizing that she seemed so unconcerned about where he was going.

He took a seat in the pew with Gram and Luke in the adult class. Quickly he became immersed in David's lesson. The minister encouraged everyone to ask questions, and the discussion went beyond surface issues.

When the bell rang to end class, Jake got up to bring Meggie in for the song service. His heart gave a sudden lurch when he spotted Sara and Will two pews behind him. He nodded in passing, but hurried on up the aisle when he noticed Meggie's teacher bringing out her class.

"How'd she do?" he asked, as Meggie threw herself into his arms.

"She did really well. I think she liked it. It takes them a little time to adjust, but she didn't cry at all. That's a good sign."

Meggie waved good-bye to the teacher and looked around as Jake carried her back to his seat. She liked the singing, and to Jake's surprise, she stayed quiet through the closing prayer.

Before the service ended, David invited everyone to adjourn to the fellowship hall to celebrate the eightieth birthday of one of their members. Gram offered to serve the cake and ice cream, so Jake had no choice but to stay.

"Meggie, want some cake and ice cream?" Luke asked, holding his arms out to her.

She reached for her uncle. "I-ceam!"

Jake laughed and handed her to his brother. "Yeah, you can go with Uncle Luke. And he can clean you up afterwards."

Luke made a face at him, and Jake watched the two of them head up the aisle. Just inside the fellowship hall, Luke and Meggie caught up with Sara and Will. Their words drifted back to Jake.

"Hi, sweet Meggie," Will said. "You going to get ice cream? Can I go with you and Uncle Luke?"

Meggie nodded and looked at Sara. "Sawa comin'?"

Jake saw Sara smile at Meggie and look back at him. "I am. But first I'm going to talk to your daddy, okay?"

" 'Kay."

Jake stood at the doorway of the sanctuary, his heart hammering in his chest. Now was his chance to apologize. What better place than a church, he thought fleetingly, as he strode across the foyer to join Sara at the door to the fellowship hall.

He took a deep breath. "Sara. I was hoping for a chance to talk to you."

She arched an eyebrow and smiled. "Oh? So was I. Wanting to talk to you."

"I'm sorry for upsetting you the other night. I was wrong—"

"Jake." Sara held up her hand and shook her head. "Do you still want to call that truce?"

"If we're going to live in the same town, I think it would be a good idea." Could she really be considering a truce after the way he'd hurt her on Sunday night? "What do you want?"

"What do I want?" Sara repeated his question and paused. She looked around at all the friends and family they shared. She smiled, seeing Luke help Meggie with her ice cream. And she saw Gina glancing their way from across the room.

"I think it might be easier to tell you what I don't want."

Jake nodded. "All right."

"I don't want our friends and family, especially your sweet Meggie, to feel the tension we feel. I don't want them to be uncomfortable every time the two of us are around." Sara looked him straight in the eyes. "And I don't want to rehash the past to get to that point."

Jake couldn't believe she was willing to bury the past and what he'd said the other night. He'd accused her of being untrue to him, he'd called her husband a liar, yet here she was offering to forget it all and go on.

"Jake? What don't you want?"

He never wanted to forget this moment. "I don't want to go back. I'd like to go forward, but do you think we can?"

Sara tilted her head to the side. "We won't know until we try, will we?"

Jake was ready to try. More than ready. He was tired of the past. All it had ever done was pull him down. He nodded. "No, we won't."

"Truce?" Sara asked, sticking out her hand.

Jake covered her small hand with both of his. "Truce."

They smiled at each other for several seconds before Sara gently pulled her hand from his. The tension between them was by no means gone, but there was a subtle difference to it.

John walked up to them, a plate of cake and ice cream in his hand. "What are you two discussing so seriously over here? World peace?"

They both chuckled, and Jake shook his head. "No. Just our little corner of it."

"Cake looks good. I think I'll go try it myself," Sara said. "Catch you two later."

Jake watched her walk over to the cake table, then scanned the room for Luke and Meggie. He nudged his cousin, and they both laughed. Luke was letting Meggie feed him, and from the looks of it, he was the one who'd need his face cleaned when the evening was over.

❧

Sara took her plate from Gram and turned to find Gina at her elbow.

"Come on. I have a spot all picked out for us."

Sara knew she was going to be quizzed on her and Jake's conversation, but at least Gina waited to bring up the topic until after they'd taken seats off in a corner where, hopefully, they wouldn't be disturbed.

"So. . .how'd it go?"

"Truce is called and hopefully we'll be able to co-exist in the same town without all of you wishing we'd both move away." Sara grinned at Gina and took a large bite of cake.

"Nah, before we'd get to that point, we'd probably lock the two of you in a room together. Or knock your heads together."

Sara chuckled. "Well, maybe you won't have to resort to those tactics now."

"You look better all ready."

"I thought about what you said. You were right."

"Only because experience taught me a few things."

Sara knew Gina was referring to her own relationship with David and how the couple had been forced to deal with a past of their own before they found happiness together. "Well, just don't expect Jake and me to turn out the way you and David did."

"No?"

Sara wasn't happy about the way her heart sped up at the thought of a future with Jake. That was not what this truce was about. "No. You can't compare Jake and me to you and David."

"You think not?" Gina quirked an eyebrow and nodded across the room to where Jake was sitting.

Sara looked up to find Jake's gaze on her. Her breath caught in her throat as he smiled, and it felt like a hundred butterflies were let loose against her ribs. She smiled back before turning around to answer her grinning friend. "No."

Gina chuckled. "Okay. I won't compare. I'll just sit back and watch."

nine

"Would you look at that?" Luke paused in cleaning frosting off his mouth and nudged Jake's arm.

"What?" Jake was busy wiping cake off Meggie's face and hands. Evidently forks and spoons didn't work when feeding Uncle Luke. Only hands would do.

"Gram and Will," Luke said. "He's making her take a break from serving. I thought he was getting seconds, but he was fixing a plate for Gram."

Jake turned to look across the room at the older couple. He saw Will pull out a chair for Gram and place a plate of cake and ice cream in front of her. Then he took a seat beside her and patted her back. They were either the very best of friends, or—

"Have I missed something?" Jake asked his brother.

"I think maybe we both have. Is that our grandmother blushing?"

Jake chuckled and nudged him. "Well, don't gawk at them."

"Gwalk, dada? I walk."

"I know you do, Sweetheart." Jake chuckled as he put Meggie on her feet and took her hands in his. "Let's go get you a drink."

Meggie hadn't quite gotten up the courage to let go yet, but her greatest joy was trying to walk. Jake led her past the table his grandmother was seated at, and a quick glance told him that the older woman's cheeks did appear to be a little rosier than usual.

Jake helped Meggie climb up the steps to the toddler fountain and held her while she drank. The thought that Gram and Will might be sweet on each other didn't really bother Jake. It did create one more reason that he and Sara needed to make their truce work. But just because they'd called a truce didn't mean everything would be smooth sailing from here on out. He was sure that he and Sara would go out of their way to keep from making the people they cared about feel uncomfortable in their presence. Who knew? Maybe one day they wouldn't feel so tense around each other. But it wasn't going to happen until he could find a way to curb the attraction he felt for her.

Watching Sara and Gina deep in conversation, Jake admitted to himself that past or no past, he was attracted to her. And he knew it wouldn't matter if he had never met Sara before—he'd still be drawn to her. Yes, she was beautiful, but there was more. There was a depth to her that hadn't always been there; a light that seemed to come from deep inside. Suddenly Jake knew that her relationship with the Lord set Sara apart and gave her the peace he so desperately wanted.

 ❧

Sara watched Jake walk Meggie to the water fountain and help her get a drink.

"He is crazy about that baby, isn't he?" Gina asked.

"He certainly is." Sara nodded. She loved watching Jake with Meggie. The love shining from his eyes when he looked at his daughter was so strong it was almost tangible. "It was just the two of them until he moved back here, and I think he's had a little bit of trouble letting others help him with her. Not that you'd know it to hear Nora talk."

"Oh? Nora isn't happy about Jake being back?"

Sara shook her head. "She thinks he came back just so he could dump Meggie on Gram, to hear her tell it." Sara instantly felt sorry for gossiping about her mother-in-law. "I shouldn't have said that. I'm sure she is just concerned about Gram taking on too much."

"Maybe that's what all of that was about, earlier." Gina looked thoughtful as she scooped up a bite of cake.

"What are you talking about, Gina? What happened?"

"Well, Nora was serving earlier, and when she saw you and

Jake talking, she said something to Ellie, and I heard Ellie tell her that it wasn't any of her business. Then Nora left in a huff."

"I'd wondered where she was. She probably won't be happy with me. I've upset her several times over Jake. I guess this is another one."

"Sara, you can't let Nora bother you. You and Jake are part of the same family, just as Nora is. Getting along is a good thing. It makes life easier on everyone."

"I know. I just don't like upsetting her." She chuckled. "Grandpa and Gram think she needs a man in her life."

"Ah, that explains what those two have their heads together about. They're hatching a plan to get Nora together with someone?"

"Well, now, it might have something to do with Nora, and it might not. I've been wondering about those two." Sara shook her head and grinned. "Don't they make an adorable couple?"

Gina laughed and nodded her head. "They do. My word, David and I go away for a month and come back to all kinds of matchmaking."

"Don't hold your breath to see if any of it is successful. Far as I know, those two haven't come up with anyone for Nora."

"What's this about someone for Nora?" Lydia asked, coming up behind them. "What a good idea!"

Sara and Gina both laughed.

"Grandpa and Gram seem to think so," Sara said. "We think that may be what they are talking about over there." She unobtrusively motioned to the table where the older couple was seated.

"Oh." Lydia sounded disappointed. "I thought maybe there was a romance brewing between those two."

"I wouldn't rule that out yet, either." Sara gathered up her plate and cup and led the way toward the kitchen to help with cleanup. "We've been wondering the very same thing."

✥

The next few days gave the tentative truce a chance to work. Jake and Sara smiled hesitantly at each other in the grocery store and waved at each other from across the street. It felt like progress when they graduated from trying not to make eye contact to actual conversation during the next few days.

On Thursday, Jake was just entering the diner as Sara began to leave. He held the door open for her. "Good morning, Sara," he said. "Nice day we're having."

"Good morning, Jake," Sara answered. "Yes, it is."

The next afternoon Jake was leaving just as she and Gina entered Deana's.

"Good afternoon, ladies," Jake said. "How are you both today?"

"Doing well, Jake," Gina answered.

"That's great. Thank you for the names you gave Gram. She said she was sure she could pick one or two girls to help out from the list you gave her." He turned to Sara and grinned. "And you, Sara? Have you had a good day?"

"Hi, Jake. I'm just fine. How are you? And Meggie and Gram, how are they?" Sara couldn't help it. She chuckled at their exaggerated politeness.

"We're doing just fine, thank you." His deep chuckle joined hers as he walked out the door.

Sara was still smiling when she took her seat across from Gina.

"Looks like the truce is holding," Gina said.

"Well, I don't think it's been tested yet. We've only seen each other in passing."

"You're both laughing at the situation. That's always a good sign."

"A sign of what?"

"Oh, come on, Sara. You two genuinely like each other. You always have."

Sara couldn't argue with her friend on that one. She and Jake had always liked each other. They'd been relaxed around each other whether they were talking or silent, and she did miss that closeness. Sara was relieved when the waitress interrupted their conversation. She didn't want to talk about her present feelings about Jake. She wasn't quite ready to admit how strong they were—even to herself.

But she did want to know about these helpers for Gram, and after the waitress left with their order, Sara turned her attention to Gina. "What's this about a helper for Gram? Is she having problems keeping up with Meggie? I offered to help anytime." If they were looking into others lending a hand, apparently Jake didn't want to take her up on her offer.

"Now don't get all riled up, Sara. From what Ellie told me, she still doesn't think she needs help. But Jake insisted she get someone. They finally compromised on getting one or two of the teens from church to come in after school to help out, at least until Jake gets into his own place and can hire a housekeeper."

"I could help out easily," Sara said. Some truce they were going to have if Jake didn't even trust her with his daughter.

"Sara, you know how independent Ellie is. She only agreed to this plan because she knows there are several girls who could use the money. It's her way of helping out. You know if it was more than a few hours a day or if she was sick or something like that, you're probably the first person she'd call."

Sara nodded. Gina was right and she was sure that Gram would call her. What she wasn't sure about was that Jake would ask her to help.

That same afternoon, she'd agreed to meet with Gram again to firm up some of the plans for the reunion. Truce or no truce, she was a little apprehensive as she knocked on the door and breathed a sigh of relief when Gram answered.

"Come in, Dear. Meggie is down for a nap, and I'm just putting a roast on for supper." She led the way back to the kitchen and poured Sara a cup of coffee.

Gram finished browning the large roast and slipped it into the oven before joining Sara at the table. She gathered her lists together, looked through her glasses at Sara, and smiled. "Let's see, where did we leave off?"

The rest of the afternoon flew by as they made more phone

calls and went over menus and shopping lists. Gram was as excited as a child about the coming reunion. They worked steadily until male banter and laughter alerted them that Jake and Luke were entering the kitchen.

"Sara! It's nice to see you," Luke said, crossing the kitchen to give his grandmother and Sara a kiss on the cheek.

Jake barely had time to smile at her before a squeal was heard from upstairs and he rushed to check on Meggie.

"Oh my, it's later than I thought," Gram said, looking at the clock. "Sara, why don't you call Will and tell him to come on over? This roast is big enough for all of us, and I just didn't seem to know when to stop peeling potatoes."

Sara noticed several more pots on the stove and realized Gram must have finished her meal preparations while she had been tied up on the phone. "That's all right, Gram. I'll go home. Grandpa may have already started supper."

The older woman picked up the phone. "Well, there's only one way to find out." She dialed the number just as Jake came back down the stairs with Meggie on his hip.

"Will, it's Ellie. Darlin', I'm afraid I've kept Sara here too long today. I've asked her and you, of course, to eat with us, but she was afraid you might have started supper already."

Apparently both Luke and Jake caught the change in their grandmother's tone as she talked to Sara's grandfather. Luke raised an eyebrow in Sara's direction and motioned toward Gram. Jake looked on as Sara shrugged and grinned. Luke raised and lowered both eyebrows as they heard Gram's side of the conversation continue.

"I'll tell her. We'll be eating in about a half hour. We'll be looking for you."

Sara quickly hid her smile as Gram turned to her. "Your grandpa said he hadn't started a thing and he'd be glad to give you a break from cooking. He'll be right over." She looked down at her apron and reached up to fluff her hair. "Sara dear, would you check the roast? I need to go freshen up just a bit."

Luke, Sara, and even Jake could barely contain their

chuckles until they were sure Gram was out of earshot.

"Did you hear that? Gram sounded all of sixteen on the phone," Jake said.

"From the sound of it, we may have to ask your grandfather what his intentions are," Luke added.

"Don't you dare embarrass those two wonderful people!" Sara said, but her giggles increased.

Meggie looked from her daddy to her uncle Luke to Sara and back again. Finally she giggled and clapped her hands, not wanting to miss out on any of the fun.

All three adults struggled to get their laughter under control before Gram came back downstairs, but they were still chuckling when she returned.

"My, my, I haven't heard this much laughter in a long time," she said as she entered the kitchen. She'd changed into a dress, put on lipstick, and coaxed her hair into soft silver waves around her face. "What has everyone's tickle bone turned on?"

Jake seemed to recover first. "Oh, Meggie got tickled about something and it just snowballed. You know how that goes. One person giggles, then another, and pretty soon, you have a whole roomful of people laughing and no one can tell you why."

"You look awfully nice, Gram. You wouldn't be sprucing up for any reason we need to know about, would you?" Luke asked.

Sara shook her head at him. What was he doing? Trying to embarrass Gram? How she and Grandpa felt about each other was none of their business.

"Lucas, I do not feel that question deserves an answer other than the obvious one. We have company coming for supper." She turned from the stove and arched an eyebrow at her youngest grandson. "Do I need any other reason to comb my hair and put a clean dress on?"

Jake and Sara couldn't help chuckling again, only this time their amusement was brought on by the look on Luke's face as he realized his grandmother had just put him in his place.

"Uh, no, Ma'am, you don't." He crossed the room and kissed her cheek to make amends. "You look quite lovely, too."

"Thank you. Now you can mash the potatoes."

Luke saluted and rolled up his sleeves. "Yes, Ma'am. I'll get on that right away."

Gram grinned at him. "Good."

Her attention turned to Jake and Sara. "Jake, will you sharpen the carving knife for me?"

"Yes, Ma'am," Jake said, plopping Meggie in her playpen until suppertime.

"And, Sara, would you be a dear and set the table in the dining room?"

The three exchanged glances and tried to hide their smiles as they went about the chores they'd been given, feeling properly disciplined.

A few minutes later, Sara stood back and looked at the table. It looked nice. The doorbell rang, and Gram called out, "Sara dear, please let your grandfather in."

Sara hurried to do just that, wondering if her grandpa had taken the time to spruce himself up as well. She opened the door and caught a strong whiff of his aftershave. She'd never seen him look so nice except for when he went to church. While he didn't have a suit on this evening, he'd dressed in a nice pair of slacks and a white shirt. His hair was slicked back, and his bushy white eyebrows actually looked tamed. He'd even trimmed his moustache. *Oh my, this does look serious.*

"Why, Grandpa, don't you look nice."

"Thank you, Darlin'." He looked around. "Where's Ellie? In the back?" Not waiting for an answer, he headed for the kitchen. Sara followed, a half smile on her lips. Grandpa seemed to feel even more at home here than she did. She noticed Gram blush as Grandpa walked over to her and took her hand in his.

"Ellie," he said, "thank you so much for inviting Sara and myself to supper."

Gram reached up and patted his cheek with her free hand. "You're very welcome, William."

They stood looking into each other's eyes until Luke called from by the stove, "Mashed potatoes are ready, Gram."

"Oh." Gram turned her attention to getting the meal on the table. "Yes, well, Jake, you get Meggie set up in the dining room. Luke, carry those potatoes in, please. And Sara dear, please get the rolls from the oven."

They all jumped to do Gram's bidding, feeling a little like intruders waiting to see what the older couple was going to do next. It wasn't until they'd reached the dining room and taken their seats that the three realized their respective grandparents were still in the kitchen. They looked at one another. The silence was deafening.

Several minutes passed before Gram led Grandpa out to the dining room. He put the nicely sliced roast in the center of the table before pulling out Gram's chair for her.

The relief was almost tangible when Meggie broke the silence by clapping her hands. "I hungry, Gma!"

"Will, would you please say grace, so we can feed this baby?"

"Dear Father, we thank You for this food we are about to eat, for those who prepared it, for this family and these friends. We thank You for watching over us and seeing to our needs daily. In Jesus' name. Amen."

Jake quickly dished up some mashed potatoes and watched as his daughter filled her spoon. She managed to take her first bite without spilling any. And her second. It looked like his daughter had finally conquered using a spoon. "Meggie, you did it!"

Meggie put down her spoon and clapped her hands. From then on the evening was hers. She flirted and giggled between each bite. But as soon as she finished eating, she reached out to Sara.

"Sawa, hode."

When Sarah looked at Jake for permission to hold his

daughter, he knew he'd never be able to deny her. He unbuckled Meggie and started to hand her to Sara, but Meggie said, "I walk."

Jake put her on her feet and steadied her. Meggie held on to his hands for a second and then let go. Everyone at the table silently watched Sara get out of her chair and kneel on the floor, holding her hands out to Meggie. Then, hands outstretched, Meggie took one. . .two. . .three steps straight into Sara's arms.

Sara hugged her. "Meggie, you did it! What a big girl you are!"

Meggie had to walk back to her daddy and then take turns walking to everyone else at the table while Uncle Luke took pictures. But she ended right back with Sara when she tired of showing off.

"Sawa, hode now."

It was impossible for Jake to keep his eyes off Meggie and Sara. Like it or not, they'd bonded to each other. It didn't bother Jake as much as it had when he'd first returned to town. Sara was wonderful with his daughter. She finished the rest of her meal with Meggie sitting in her lap as if she belonged there. When she brushed the hair from Meggie's cheek and kissed her, Jake was reminded of the night she'd put Meggie to bed. The night he'd held her in his arms and kissed her. His gaze strayed to her mouth, and he looked up to see color stealing up her face as her eyes met his. Was she remembering too? He liked the thought that she might be.

Meggie seemed content to stay right where she was, and Jake couldn't blame her. When the meal was over, the only thing that got her out of Sara's lap was the promise of a horsy ride from Uncle Luke. Sara insisted on clearing the table and doing the dishes, leaving Gram and her grandfather to visit while Jake and Luke played with Meggie.

It wasn't until Sara and her grandfather had left and Jake was upstairs giving Meggie her bath that he realized he was no closer to knowing how serious his grandmother and Will were about each other than he'd been before supper. While he'd meant to pay special attention to how they reacted to each other during the meal, it seemed his focus had been elsewhere. His attention had been taken by his daughter. . .and by Will's granddaughter.

❧

Sara was tired but still too keyed up for sleep. She made some hot chocolate and took it to the front porch. Setting the swing in motion, she smiled, thinking back on the evening. The truce had held and she was glad. She and Jake had done the right thing by agreeing to it.

Now if she could just find a way to keep her heart from going into overdrive every time she was around him. Sara sighed and closed her eyes, but all she could see was the look in Jake's eyes while she held Meggie. She hoped that hadn't been pity she'd seen, because pity was the last thing she wanted from him. She couldn't deny it anymore. She was falling in love with Jake all over again.

ten

Jake sat in Meggie's room, still rocking the baby long after she'd fallen asleep and thinking back over the evening. After the awkwardness before Gram and Will came into the dining room, the evening had been a true delight. Now that she had let go of his fingers and gone off by herself, his daughter was officially a toddler.

He was actually glad she'd taken those first steps to Sara. He'd been able to watch them both, and it'd been hard to tell who'd been more excited, Meggie or Sara.

The truce was holding, and he was pleased, even with the stipulation to stay away from the past. There were only two reasons he'd ever want to visit those days again—to find out if Sara had truly loved him and to explain about Melissa.

But as he looked down at his sleeping child, Jake wasn't sure he could do that. Melissa had given him Meggie. And telling Sara that he suspected Melissa's first pregnancy might not have been genuine—that it actually was a trick to get him to the altar—seemed disloyal to the mother of his child. Not to mention that it would seem that he was laying the blame for the end of his relationship with Sara at someone else's feet, when he knew it was the result of his own choices.

For years he'd blamed Sara, Wade, and Melissa for messing up his life. How wrong he'd been. He was the one who had been so hot-headed that night that he'd refused to listen to Sara. He was the one who'd gone against all he'd been taught when he got back to college that night. Jake groaned in disgust with himself and nearly woke his sleeping child.

He stood up and carried Meggie to her crib. Laying her down gently, he patted her on the back to keep her asleep.

He propped his elbow on Meggie's crib and buried his face

in his hands. *Oh, God, please forgive me for blaming others for the mistakes I've made. Please help me to truly take responsibility for the pain I've caused them and to mend my relationship with You. I'm not even sure how to go about it, so I just ask You to show me the way. In Jesus' name. Amen.*

Jake bent down to brush his lips over Meggie's brow, thanking the Lord for blessing him with this child.

❧

Sara was enjoying her second cup of coffee when Nora called the next morning. Somehow she knew it would be her mother-in-law before she answered the phone.

"Sara dear, I called last night but you weren't at home."

"No, Grandpa and I were at Gram's. I'd been helping her with—"

"With that baby. I knew she would be too much for Ellie."

"No, Nora. It wasn't Meggie. We were working on the reunion. We lost track of time and Gram asked Grandpa and me to eat supper with them." Sara wished she didn't constantly feel the need to explain everything to Nora.

"Oh. I see. And I suppose Jake was there too?"

"Yes, he and Luke were both there."

"I see."

Sara didn't like the condescending tone her mother-in-law was using. "No, Nora, I don't think—"

"Sara, remember, I warned you about Jake. I saw him seek you out Wednesday night. He's got his sights on you as a mother for Meggie."

"Nora, Jake does not have his sights set on me." Sara knew her voice sounded as irritated as she felt, but she couldn't help it. Sara trembled just at the thought of being married to Jake and becoming Meggie's mommy. But having to hide those feelings from Nora and everyone else wasn't easy. And Sara knew it wasn't going to get any easier.

As if she sensed Sara's mood, Nora quickly changed her tone. "I'm sorry, Dear, I just don't want to see you hurt. I want the best for you, you know that."

"I do know that, Nora. But Jake has moved back here. He's part of the family. You can't pretend he doesn't exist."

"Yes, well, I don't have to condone his dumping his child on Ellie."

"Nora, Jake has not dumped Meggie on anyone. He's hiring several of the teens from church to come in and help out. And I think he had to talk Gram into agreeing on that. Has it ever occurred to you that she's enjoying keeping Meggie?"

"I'm sure she's a joy. But Ellie isn't getting any younger."

Remembering the tenderness Nora had shown with Meggie, Sara sighed and shook her head. Maybe Nora was truly concerned about everyone. If so, it was a shame that she never came across that way.

"You're right, she isn't. But she's enjoying herself right now, and that's a blessing." Sara changed the subject. "How are you feeling, Nora? Have you been back to the doctor to get the results from your tests?"

"I'm fine. Just under a lot of stress, as if I didn't already know that. You know what kind of year it's been. I don't know why everyone expects me to act as if life is just rosy and I have no cares."

"Nora, no one expects that from you."

"Yes, well, Dr. Wellington seems to think I've grieved quite long enough. He had the audacity to tell me to find another doctor so that he would feel free to ask me out."

"Oh my." Sara grinned. Maybe Gram and Grandpa weren't needed in the matchmaking department after all.

"Well, I have no intentions of going out with the man."

"I've heard he's very nice, Nora. Gina thinks the world of him. And it'd be nice for you to get out occasionally."

"I'm too old for all of that dating nonsense."

"Nora, you aren't too old at all."

"Well, when you've been a widow as long as I have, then we'll see how old you feel."

Suddenly Sara's life, as Nora painted it, loomed out in front of her. . .long and lonely. Just as suddenly, she knew she didn't want to settle for being alone the rest of her life. She wanted a home and family. She wanted someone to love and take care of.

But there was no way she could tell Nora that. No way at all.

જ

David's sermon that Sunday focused once again on trusting the Lord to forgive and then demonstrating that trust by forgiving ourselves and going forward instead of dwelling on any past wrongdoings.

Jake wondered if David might be preaching straight at him, because he'd never thought about forgiveness in quite that way before. He knew that he'd had a hard time forgiving himself and forgetting the past. Sometimes he wondered how God could love him after he'd strayed from all he'd believed and been taught.

He sought David out the next morning, showing up at his office with coffee and donuts.

"Does that offer to talk still stand?" he asked, waving the bag of donuts across the desk.

David laughed. "Sure does. It'd stand even if you didn't have something delicious in that bag. Come on in and sit down."

After they'd downed a couple donuts and most of the coffee, David leaned back in his chair and got to the point. "What do you want to talk about, my friend?"

Jake leaned forward and clasped his hands together. "I liked your lesson yesterday. About forgiveness."

"I'm glad. Was there anything particular about it you'd like to discuss?" David pulled his Bible to the center of the desk.

"The part about forgiving ourselves, forgetting the past, being. . .an act of trust?"

David nodded. "Many of us have problems with that. Sometimes it's hard for us to believe we're truly forgiven even after we've asked for that very thing."

"That verse you quoted from Philippians—"

"Philippians 3:13–15," David said as he opened his Bible

and flipped through the pages. *"'Brothers, I do not consider myself yet to have taken hold of it. But one thing I do: Forgetting what is behind and straining toward what is ahead, I press on toward the goal to win the prize for which God has called me heavenward in Christ Jesus. All of us who are mature should take such a view of things. And if on some point you think differently, that too God will make clear to you.'* Is that it?"

Jake nodded. "That's it. I know I've dwelt in the past way too much. I'm tired of it weighing me down."

"Sounds to me like you're just about there, Jake." David chuckled. "Maybe God's making it all clear to you."

"I certainly hope so. It's about time I figured it out, don't you think?"

"Well, I was a late bloomer myself," David said. "Sadly, it seems to take some of us longer than others."

He got up and refilled their Styrofoam cups from a coffee pot he had set up in the corner. "How are you and Sara doing? Gina mentioned something about a truce being called."

"Ah, well, we decided it was time to try to get along. This town isn't going to grow so large that we can keep from running into one another. And we have the same family and friends."

"Want to talk about why you two feel so uncomfortable around each other?"

"Nah, it's in that past I'm trying to get past." Jake grinned.

"Yeah, Gina and I had one of those kinds of pasts ourselves." David nodded. "We did have to visit it a time or two before we were able to forgive each other."

Jake shook his head. "One of the amendments of the truce was that we don't 'rehash the past.'"

"Your amendment or hers?"

"Hers."

"That might make it a little harder to put to rest."

Jake looked down into his coffee cup and sighed. "That's what I'm afraid of."

David shook his head. "My friend, notice I said harder. Not impossible. Take it to the Lord and let Him handle it."

Jake grinned and got to his feet. "I think I'll do just that. Thanks, old friend."

David stood up and the two men shook hands. "Any time."

❧

The Teddy Bear Brigade, as they'd taken to calling themselves, had decided to meet each Tuesday at the church for lunch and an afternoon of bear making. With one of the teens keeping watch over Meggie, Gram was free to join the group. Everyone brought their favorite dish, and David found one excuse after another to come into the fellowship hall, until finally the ladies insisted he join them for lunch.

Sara laughed, overhearing Gina admonish her husband at the same time she set a plate in front of him. "You are pitiful, you know? Taking advantage of these wonderful ladies, just because you're the minister." The sting was removed from Gina's words by the smile she bestowed upon her husband.

"I know, my love, I know." David nodded. "But you weren't in my office trying to endure the tempting smells wafting in from all this food. Why, my stomach was growling so loud I couldn't concentrate on tomorrow night's lesson."

Sara and Gram burst out laughing, and Gina just shook her head.

"Well, since you're here, would you be so kind as to say the blessing for us?"

David smiled at his wife and looked at all the ladies. "I'd be delighted. Please pray with me."

He bowed his head. "Dear Father, we thank You for all this food and for each of those who prepared it. Thank You for letting these sisters invite me to join in this meal. And thank You for the response they've had from these little bears they're making. Please continue to bless their work and each of their lives, dear Lord. In Jesus' name. Amen."

Everyone enjoyed the meal, and David even helped with the cleanup before going back to his office.

"You've got a good man there, Gina," Gram said as the ladies settled down to their sewing.

"Yes, Ma'am, I do." Gina threaded her needle. "It took us a long time to get it all together, though."

"Well, good things are usually worth the wait." Gram pinned a bear pattern to a short length of material. "How's Nora doing?" she asked Sara, changing the subject. "I haven't heard from her in several days."

Sara shook her head. "I'm not real sure. She had an appointment with that new doctor in town—"

"Dr. Wellington?" Gina asked. "He's supposed to be a very good doctor."

Gram winked at Sara. "Is he married?"

"No. He's never been married, from what I hear," Nell Schneider offered from across the table.

Sara got up and went to the kitchen, just off the fellowship hall, to put on a fresh pot of coffee. It was hard to keep from telling everyone that this Dr. Wellington was interested in her mother-in-law.

Gram followed her into the kitchen and pulled some Styrofoam cups down from the cabinet. "Might be a nice match for Nora," she whispered to Sara.

"Not if she doesn't like him," Sara whispered back.

Gina joined them in the small room. "What are you two cooking up now?" She grinned, as it seemed to dawn on her. "Oh. . .now, that might be a good match. He's very plain spoken. Doesn't impress me as the type to take much guff from anyone. He could be just the kind of man Nora needs."

Sara sighed. She couldn't keep it in any longer. "Well, we're halfway there. It seems Dr. Wellington is interested enough in Nora that he told her to find another doctor. He wants to ask her out."

Gram chuckled. "Now that does sound promising."

"Not as much as we'd like," Sara admitted. "Nora says she isn't interested."

"You think that's so?"

Sara shook her head. "I don't know. We were talking on the phone so I couldn't see her face. She says she's too old for a relationship."

"Oh, hogwash," Gram said. She went to the refrigerator and brought out some cream.

Sara grinned over at Gina. She had a feeling that would be Gram's opinion. At least it should be, if she and Grandpa were starting to care for one another.

"Maybe I'll just have me a talk with Nora," Gram continued.

"I think that's a great idea," Sara said.

"So do I," Gina added.

"I'll try to get with her in the next few days, and we'll have us a good long talk." As if that settled everything, Gram raised the service window facing the fellowship hall. "Ladies, coffee's ready."

⁂

Sara gave Gram a ride home. When they arrived, they found Meggie outside with Maria Bellows, one of the teens Jake had hired to help out. Enjoying the warm afternoon sun, Maria and Meggie sat together in the tire swing hanging from the large cottonwood tree in the backyard.

"Hi, Meggie," Sara called as Gram went inside to take care of her teddy bear supplies. "Are you having a good time?"

Meggie nodded and reached out to her. Sara dropped her purse to the ground. "Want me to swing you?"

Maria vacated the swing, and they laughed as Sara clumsily tried to seat herself in the tire swing. Once she felt halfway secure, she reached for the toddler. "Let's see if I remember how to do this."

Meggie giggled and clapped as they swung back and forth. Sara heard the back door slam but kept her eyes on the child, for fear of dropping her. "Maybe Daddy needs to look into getting a regular swing set for you," she observed.

"Daddy has been thinking the very same thing."

Sara's heart skipped more than a few beats as she recognized Jake's voice.

"Afternoon, ladies," he said, his smile taking in all three women.

"Hi, Mr. Breland. Meggie's been a really good girl this afternoon," Maria said. "If she's like this all the time, babysitting her will be a piece of cake."

Jake laughed. "Well, I can't guarantee she won't give you fits some days."

"That's all right. She's a sweetie anyway. We'll get along just fine."

"Thank you, Maria. There's a check for you on the kitchen table."

"Thanks." Maria waved to Meggie. "Bye, Meggie. I'll see you on Monday."

"Bye-bye." Meggie waved back.

"Bye, Mrs. Tanner, Mr. Breland." The young girl hurried across the lawn to get what Sara was sure was her first paycheck.

Sara let the swing gradually slow and brought it to a halt.

"Dada, hode me."

Jake took his daughter from Sara and grinned. "So, you think I should get a regular swing set?"

Sara struggled out of the swing as gracefully as she could, feeling Jake's eyes on her. She tried to ignore whatever it was that had her heart hammering against her sides. "Well, it might make it a little easier to swing her, unless. . .you know, they have those baby swings that Meggie would fit in, and you could attach it to the tree until she got big enough to sit in this one."

Jake scratched the back of his head. "Oh, yeah. I think I've seen those at the toy store. That's a good idea, Sara. I kind of hate to have to put up a swing set here, just to take it down in a few months when we move to our house."

"How's that going?" She wondered what kind of house he was going to build. Long ago they'd talked about the house they'd build some day, and she could still remember the floor plan they'd decided on.

"I'm supposed to meet with the builder tomorrow to go over some plans. Another week or two and hopefully I'll have the plans nailed down and he'll have all the subcontractors lined up."

"Jake Breland, what is this you have in my kitchen?" Gram called from the back door.

"Oh, that's my surprise for Meggie." He handed his daughter back to Sara. "I'll be right back."

He ran across the yard and into the house. When he and Gram came back out seconds later, he was carrying a large box. Sara watched as Jake knelt down and pulled an adorable golden retriever puppy from the box. Then he reached up for Meggie.

"Doggie, doggie!" Meggie said, as Jake held her close to the puppy and let her pet it.

Sara and Gram looked at each other and laughed, trying to figure out who was the most excited, Meggie, the puppy, or Jake. Gram kneeled down to pet the dog. "Now I wonder just who you bought this for, Jake—Meggie or yourself?"

Sara laughed at the injured expression on Jake's face.

"Now, Gram, you know I put my daughter's interests first." He reached down and helped his grandmother to her feet.

"Yes, I do. I'm teasing, Jake. It's a pretty dog."

"He is, isn't he?" Jake reached down and picked up Meggie while they watched the puppy run around. "We can keep it then?"

Even Meggie looked at her great-grandmother, as if she knew who had the final say.

"It can sleep in the utility room. But it stays out here during the day."

Jake grinned and bent to kiss his grandmother's cheek. "Thank you, Gram."

"Now, I'm going in to start supper." Gram smiled at Sara. "Want to stay and eat with us, Sara?"

"Thanks, Gram, but Grandpa is making stew." She reached out and tweaked Meggie's nose. "I'd better be going."

"Maybe another time," Gram said, heading for the house. "Thanks for bringing me home."

The puppy decided to run rings around the older woman, and Sara and Jake laughed as she made a game out of pretending to turn and chase it. The puppy would stop in its tracks and yap at her before running her again.

But Gram made one move a little too quickly, the puppy tumbled between her feet, and Gram tripped. Jake handed Meggie to Sara and ran toward his grandmother, but he wasn't fast enough and his grandmother landed on her ankle. By the time Sara and Meggie got there, Jake was tenderly checking Gram's foot and leg.

"I'm so sorry," he said to the injured woman. "I should never have brought that puppy home. I should have waited until Meggie and I were in our own place."

Gram patted his hand, although she was in obvious pain. "It wasn't the dog's fault, Jake. I shouldn't have been teasing it. Every once in awhile, I forget I'm nearing eighty instead of eighteen."

Jake nodded and looked at Sara. "Maybe we should call an ambulance."

"Jacob Breland, I do not need an ambulance. Just get me in the house."

"No, Gram." Jake lifted her into his arms and looked at Sara. "Would you mind watching Meggie, Sara? I think I'd better get Gram to the hospital."

"Of course I'll stay. We'll be here when you get back."

Their eyes met, sharing unspoken concerns.

Sara and Meggie watched Jake gently ease Gram into his car and take off. Sara took the baby into the house and went to the phone. She dialed her home number, all the while praying, *Dear Lord, please let there be no broken bones. Please let Gram be all right.*

eleven

After telling Grandpa about Gram's accident, Sara called the rest of the family to let them know what had happened. She was surprised when there was no answer at Nora's, but she left a message on her answering machine and hoped to hear from her later.

Grandpa came right over, bringing his Crock-Pot stew with him. But he paced so badly he made Sara even more nervous than she already was, and she finally sent him to the hospital to check on Gram.

Sara tried not to watch the clock and kept herself busy by entertaining Meggie and making her a supper of macaroni and cheese. She made sure it was cool enough before setting the bowl in front of Meggie, but when she began to fill the fork with macaroni, Meggie reached for it.

Sara relinquished the small utensil to her and chuckled as Meggie slowly forked several pieces of the cheesy pasta and deftly plopped them into her mouth.

Remembering the first day she'd watched Meggie make such a mess with finger food and a sippy cup, Sara marveled at how fast the little girl had caught on to the intricacies of feeding herself.

Grandpa called from the hospital to let her know that Gram was still waiting to see a doctor. There'd been a wreck earlier, and the doctors were tied up. He promised to call and update her as he could.

Sara had bathed Meggie and rocked her to sleep before the phone rang again. Jake was calling to update her and check on Meggie.

"How is Gram?" Sara asked. "Is anything broken?"

"Can you believe she didn't break a thing? But she does

have a nasty sprained ankle and will be down for awhile," he answered.

"Bless her heart. She's not going to like that at all."

"No, she's not a happy camper. And it's all my fault. I should never have brought that puppy home."

"Oh, Jake, I'm sure she doesn't blame you."

"No, she doesn't. But I blame myself." He changed the subject. "How's my girl? Did she give you any problems?"

Sara chuckled. "Not one. She fed herself, had a ball in the tub, and went right to sleep."

"Well, I just wanted to let you know that we'll be on our way as soon as we can get Gram released."

"Okay. I'll have supper on the table."

"You don't have to do that, Sara."

"It's no problem, Jake. Grandpa brought over the stew he had cooking. All I have to do is heat up some rolls and set the table."

"All right. Thank you, Sara, for staying with Meggie—for everything. I really appreciate it."

"You're welcome. . .hurry home. With Gram," Sara added quickly before hanging up the phone.

She set the table and put on a fresh pot of coffee. She'd just finished placing the rolls in the oven when the phone rang again. Nora had returned home and wanted to know the latest. Sara was glad that she could at least give her an updated report on Gram.

"I just got back from town," Nora said. "I wish I'd known. I could have gone to the hospital with. . .ah, to see about her."

"Well, they'll be home any minute now. I'll be sure and tell her you called to check on her," Sara said, wondering who Nora might have gone to the hospital *with*.

"Yes, please do, Dear." Nora's tone cooled slightly. "I suppose this means you'll be helping her with the baby."

"Of course I'll help, Nora."

"Yes, well, I figured as much."

Sara heard a car pull up outside. "Nora, I think they're

home now. I'll be sure and give Gram your love."

"Please do."

"I'll talk to you tomorrow and let you know how she's doing. Night, Nora." Sara hung up and ran to the door.

Her heart ached at the sight of Gram struggling to get out of the car. But she had to smile, hearing Jake try to convince his grandmother to let him carry her inside. "Gram, you have plenty of time to get used to those crutches tomorrow. Let me carry you into the house."

"No, Jake. I want to do it myself."

"Won't you let me carry you, Ellie?" Grandpa asked.

"Will, you aren't any younger than I am. You'd drop me or trip over something, and we'd both end up back at that hospital. Now both of you move out of my way. I can do this."

Sara could tell Gram was tired and hurting from the abrupt way in which she talked to two of her favorite men. They'd probably been hounding her about what she could and couldn't do all the way home. She had to chuckle as she watched Gram make her way to the back porch, with Jake and Grandpa right beside her. But as she watched the injured woman maneuver the steps on crutches, Sara was sure she knew how the two men felt. Her fingers itched to reach out and help. They breathed a collective sigh of relief when Gram made it through the back door and into the kitchen.

"Are you hungry?" Sara asked as Gram took her seat at the table.

"I am starved, Dear, thank you."

"Me too," Jake said. "The cafeteria was closed, and all they had were those awful vending machines. After you told me Will's stew was waiting, I just got hungrier." Jake chuckled. "What can I do to help?"

"You can put ice in the glasses and get the tea," Sara answered, bringing the stew to the table.

She dipped out a bowl for everyone while Jake took care of the drinks. Grandpa was busy finding an extra chair for Gram to prop her foot up on.

Once they were all seated, Jake offered the blessing and thanked the Lord that his grandmother wasn't hurt any worse.

"My, this stew is tasty, Will. Thank you. I didn't realize just how hungry I was," Gram said.

They'd barely finished eating when Luke, John, Lydia, and Ben showed up to check on Gram. Amid hugs and kisses, she tried to assure everyone she was fine, but the telltale black and blue inching up from her ankle to her calf said otherwise.

"I think I should stay here tonight, just in case you need help," Lydia offered.

Gram shook her head. "I'm perfectly capable of getting myself to bed. I don't need anyone to look after me, but I'll have to admit, I'll need some help with that little tyke upstairs."

"Don't worry about a thing, Gram. I can stay home with Meggie," Jake said.

John nodded. "He can. Or he can bring her into the office."

"I. . .I'd be glad to come over and watch Meggie. I'm only a few blocks away, and I'd love to help out, if it's all right with everyone." Sara looked at Jake to gauge his response. She wasn't sure what his quick frown was saying.

Grandpa chimed in with his two cents. "That's a good idea. Lydia would have to come in from the ranch. We live much closer, and I can come over and help out too. There's no need for Jake to stay home all day when he has all of us to lend a hand."

"This is true. No matter how we work it out, Jake, we're family and we're here to help," Lydia said.

"Well, if I have any say in all this planning, I'd like to take Sara up on her offer," Gram said. "We're in the middle of planning the reunion anyway, and Meggie has taken to her from the very first. I think she'll be happier if Sara is around."

Everyone seemed to be looking at Jake for his approval. He looked around the room and knew this was exactly why he'd come back to Sweet Springs—having family nearby to help with Meggie when he needed them. He smiled and nodded.

"Thank you all. I know Gram and Meggie will be in good

hands no matter who is with them." He hadn't expected to be turning to Sara for help, but his family would never understand if he turned down her generous offer. "If you really don't mind, Sara, I think Gram is right. Meggie will be thrilled to have you here each day."

Their eyes met, and for a brief moment he wished he could retract what he'd just said. Not because he didn't want Sara around, but because he did. He knew having her close by on a daily basis could lead to more heartache. Yet he wanted to be able to see her every day. He held his breath, waiting for her answer.

"I'll be here first thing in the morning. Just tell me what time you need me."

❧

Early the next morning Sara let herself into Gram's sunny kitchen with the key she'd been given the night before. Jake had told her she didn't need to be there before nine o'clock, but she'd awakened early and couldn't see any sense in sitting around waiting when Gram might need help with something.

She quietly put the coffee on and went upstairs to check on the patient.

"God bless you, Sara," Gram said as she entered the room. "I'm a little stiffer than I thought I'd be this morning. Could you help me get out of this bed, please?"

"Of course I can. I should have slept here last night," she said, feeling bad that she hadn't insisted on staying. She helped Gram slide her legs to the side of the bed and put an arm around her to steady her while she balanced on the crutches.

"There was no need for you to stay here last night," Gram insisted as she slowly made her way across the room. "I slept fine. That pain pill put me right out. But I've been awake for about an hour and I didn't want to wake Meggie too early by yelling for Jake to come help me."

Sara stood outside the bathroom door in case Gram needed her, but the older woman managed just fine. She refused to get back in bed, and took a seat in the easy chair beside the window.

"You know me, Sara. I can't stay in bed. In fact, once Jake is up and around, would you ask him to help me downstairs? I'll be much more comfortable there than up here."

"Gram, you really ought to rest that ankle for a few days."

"I'm going to rest it. Just not up here. I want to be down where you and Meggie are."

Sara tried to talk her into staying in bed, but Gram could be stubborn, and Sara finally gave in.

They heard a knock on the door and looked up to see Jake sticking his head around the corner. "Good morning. How are you feeling, Grams?"

Sara caught her breath at how handsome he looked first thing in the morning. He was dressed in a maroon robe, but his eyes still had that sleepy look and his jaw was dark with an overnight beard. His smile had her heart tripping over itself, and she was glad Gram answered him.

"I'll feel much better once I get downstairs," she insisted. "I'd like you to help me get there. I don't like feeling cut off from everything."

Jake raised a questioning eyebrow at Sara. She shrugged and found her voice. "I think she's going to get downstairs one way or another. The safest way would probably be for you to help her."

Jake nodded. "Can you wait until I shower, Gram?"

"Of course."

"Then I'll hurry." He looked at Sara. "I think I hear Meggie stirring. Would you mind bringing her down to her playpen in the kitchen? She's used to playing in it until I get her breakfast ready."

"I'll be glad to," Sara said. She turned back to Gram. "Do you need me to get you anything first?"

Gram shook her head. "No, I'm fine until Jake comes back to get me. You go see about our little darlin'."

Sara didn't have to be prodded to check on Meggie. She followed Jake down the hall to the baby's room and watched his grin turn into a full-fledged chuckle as Meggie looked up and greeted him. "Dada!"

Twin sets of dimples greeted each other as Jake picked up his daughter. "Mornin', Precious."

Meggie looked over his shoulder and spotted Sara for the first time. "Sawa!"

"Hi, Meggie. Can I get you ready and take you downstairs while Daddy takes his shower?"

Meggie reached out to her. Jake chuckled and kissed his daughter before handing her to Sara. "Well, I guess that answers your question."

"I think we're going to get along just fine, Jake. Don't you worry about us." Sara took Meggie over to the changing table and set about getting the baby ready to go downstairs.

"No, I won't," Jake said. He turned to the hall. "I'll be down to get her breakfast ready as soon as I get cleaned up and get Gram down there so she can oversee everything."

But by the time he got downstairs with Gram, Sara had bacon and eggs on the table and Meggie was in her chair, nibbling on toast and bacon.

"Oh, this is nice, Sara," Gram said as she shifted to get comfortable in her chair and prop her foot up on a small footstool Jake had found.

"Yes, it is," he said, taking his seat next to Meggie.

"I wasn't sure what to feed Meggie," Sara said, pouring three cups of coffee and taking a seat across from Jake. "I thought she could probably handle this."

Jake spooned some scrambled eggs onto Meggie's plate and handed her the small fork she liked. "This is fine. She loves bacon."

Sara sat back with her cup of coffee and watched Jake lift four pieces of bacon onto his plate. "And I can see her daddy does too."

Jake chuckled and nodded. "She comes by it honestly."

"Tomorrow, have Will come on over for breakfast," Gram said. "No sense in him having to cook for himself while we're all enjoying each other's company."

"Yes, do," Jake added. "We've taken his cook away from him, the least we can do is have him join us."

"Grandpa doesn't mind. He—"

"Is a good man. But there's no sense messing up two kitchens when one will do," Gram said with a tone of finality.

Sara grinned and looked at Jake. He shrugged and nodded. "I'll be sure and ask him to come with me tomorrow, Gram. I'm sure he'll be showing up anytime now, anyway."

"Oh, Jake," Gram said, changing the subject, "before you go to work, did you buy any dog food?"

"It's in the back of my car. I'll be sure and get it before I leave." He looked at his grandmother. "If you're sure about keeping him. I really do feel badly, Gram."

A small whine was heard, and they looked up to see the puppy looking through the screen door. Meggie clapped her hands. "Doggie, doggie!"

"Now, how could I tell you to get rid of that puppy after that?" Gram asked. She shook her head. "I told you it wasn't the puppy's fault. Of course he can stay."

"Thanks, Gram." He went outside and was back in just a few minutes. "I fed the dog and gave him water, too. Do you need anything brought back down from upstairs?"

"No, my medicine is in my pocket, the crutches are right here—"

"And I'm here if she thinks of anything she needs," Sara added.

"And you're the only reason I can even think of going to work today. Thank you, Sara." Jake smiled at her from across the room.

"You're welcome. I'm glad I can help. I've had a lot of it given to me from this family."

Jake nodded and headed upstairs. He came back down only minutes later with a jacket slung over his shoulder. He kissed the top of Gram's head, "You take it easy today, you hear?"

"I will."

He bent down and kissed Meggie on the cheek. "You be a

good girl for Sara, okay?"

Meggie nodded. " 'Kay."

Jake straightened and looked over at Sara, wishing he could kiss her too. "I'll see you this evening. If you need anything, just call the office."

"I will." Sara smiled and nodded, motioning toward the door. "Shoo, Jake. We'll be just fine. I promise."

And they were. Grandpa came over and entertained Gram for most of the day, making sure she took a nap both morning and afternoon. While she slept, he took Meggie out to play with the puppy so that Sara could straighten up the upstairs rooms and do some wash.

The phone rang on and off all day with relatives, church members, and townspeople wanting to know how Gram was and offering to help in any way they could. By noon, Sara knew not to start supper, because several of the ladies from church were arranging to bring over a series of meals. The outpouring of care and concern for Gram reminded Sara of how lucky she felt to be part of such a wonderful church family.

But the best part of the day was, without a doubt, Meggie. Sara loved interacting with the toddler. At nap time, Meggie came to Sara with her blankie and crawled into her lap. Holding the baby close and rocking her, Sara envisioned her own child being cuddled close and rocked to sleep in heaven. She gathered Meggie just a little closer as the pain she always carried eased.

twelve

The next week flew by for Sara as she tried to see that Gram took it easy and worked to keep up with Meggie. Sara kept her camera close by so she could get snapshots of an adorable Meggie toddling around, falling, and picking herself up.

Gram's ankle seemed to turn a different color each day. It went through varying shades of black, blue, and green before settling into a yellowish gray. But as always, the older woman's attitude inspired Sara. Gram didn't let the pain or the awkward use of crutches keep her down. Sara could only hope she'd be as full of life and living when she neared eighty.

While Meggie napped, she and Gram either worked on the plans for the reunion, or sewed and stuffed more teddy bears. Meggie woke up early one afternoon, and Sara brought her down to her playpen in the kitchen while she finished up one of the bears.

"Wat dat?" Meggie asked, pointing to the little bear.

"It's a bear, Sweetie." Sara made one last stitch, tied it off, and cut the thread. She carried the brightly checkered bear over and showed it to Meggie. "Do you like it?"

Meggie dropped the blanket she'd been holding and grabbed the little stuffed animal. "Thanky, Sawa."

Sara's heart melted and she wondered why she'd never given the child one before. "You're welcome, Sweetie."

Sara drove home unsure of which time of day she liked best lately. The mornings when she let herself in the back door, brought Meggie down, and started breakfast while Jake showered, dressed, and helped Gram get downstairs. Or the evenings, when he came home from work and they all ate supper at the big table in the kitchen.

She had no doubts about which part she liked least. She

hated leaving at night. She always felt as if she'd left a big chunk of herself back at Gram's. As she pulled into the driveway at home, she was pretty certain it was her heart she'd left behind.

The next morning, Sara was delighted to see both Jake and Meggie already downstairs when she let herself in the back door. Jake had the coffee on and was holding Meggie on his hip while he stirred something on the stove. The little girl grinned widely when Sara greeted her.

"Sawa!" She held up the little bear Sara had given her the day before. "Ted-bear seep wif me."

"He did?" Sara looked around for the child's blanket and, finding no evidence of it, looked questioningly at Jake.

"It appears Meggie has given up her blankie for Ted-bear. She slept with him all night and had him clasped in her arms when I went in to get her this morning."

"Oh, how sweet. I kind of hate to see the blanket go, though."

Jake chuckled. "I know. She didn't even ask for it last night when I rocked her to sleep. But thank you for giving her the bear. She loves it."

He turned back to the oatmeal he was cooking for his daughter and poured out a bowl. "This just needs to cool. Would you mind taking Meggie while I go up and help Gram down? I'm meeting with the builder to finalize the house plans this morning."

"Of course I don't mind." Sara reached out and took Meggie into her arms. "Hi, Sweetie. You ready to eat?"

"Ted-bear eat too?"

"Hmm," Sara said to herself as she settled Meggie into her high chair. "I can see that we might need a spare bear around here. I'll see if we have enough of that material left to make another one."

By the end of the day, Meggie had a spare bear in her room, but she still hadn't asked for her blanket.

Jake came home from work that night with the plans to his

and Meggie's new home under his arm. The rest of the family had been invited over to take a look, but they all had to wait until after supper when the table was cleared to get a look at them.

Jake spread the plans out on the table, stood back, and waited for comments. He answered question after question about this room and that. Then he noticed Sara looking intently at the plans, color flooding her face. She bit her bottom lip. Suddenly he realized what he had done. His plans matched exactly the plans he and Sara had talked about when they were young. He hadn't even been aware that he'd duplicated them.

The house would be a large two-story with a wide wraparound porch. The kitchen stood along one end with windows on the front, side, and back of the house. He remembered how Sara had commented years ago that she wanted to be able to look out and see their children playing no matter where she was in the house.

This house would have nooks and crannies much like Gram's house—all the little touches that builders usually didn't bother with anymore but that gave a house character. The same touches he and Sara had decided they wanted when they were young and in love. Suddenly he remembered that years ago he and Sara had walked along the very block where he was now building and how he had commented that he'd like to build a house there some day.

"I like it, Bro," Luke said, bringing Jake out of his reverie.

"So do I. It's going to look especially good on that block. It'll look as though it's been there forever," John said. "It'll blend right in."

"It's going to be a lovely home for you and Meggie, Jake," Lydia agreed.

Jake was glad they all liked it, but he knew there was truly only one opinion that mattered to him.

Sara turned to him with a smile. "Well, it goes without saying that I love it."

That was the only reference she made that came close to touching on its similarities to their dream house, but it was enough to make Jake realize that his dream home wouldn't be complete without Sara in it. He wanted them back together. Not just as friends. While he'd been crazy about the younger Sara, he was head over heels in love with this one.

He looked into her eyes. "I was hoping you'd like it," he said, but his mind skittered all over the place. How could he let Sara know that he'd loved her all his life, without feeling disloyal to Meggie's mother? Was it possible that he ever could? Jake didn't know how much he could reveal to Sara about his and Melissa's relationship, but he did know one thing. He was in love with Sara, he wanted her in his and Meggie's life, and he was going to do everything in his power to make her see they truly were meant for each other.

Jake went to bed that night with a new determination. He was going to try to get Sara to fall in love with him again. He knew he was putting his heart on the line, but he also knew that he had no choice. He loved Sara, plain and simple. Now he just had to do his best to convince her they were meant to be together.

ઽ

The first phase of Jake's plan went into action the next morning. He didn't have to do much talking to convince his grandmother and Will that Sara needed a break. But he knew persuading Sara might be a different story. So he did the only thing he could think of. He called Gina and David and enlisted their aid.

Jake dawdled over breakfast that morning so long that finally Sara asked him if he was taking the day off.

"No. But I can if you need me here to do anything."

"No, Jake, we're coping very well. I'm just not used to you being here after nine o'clock. Are you feeling all right?"

"Sara, I'm fine. I just wasn't in a hurry today. Actually, I—"

The phone rang right on cue and Jake answered it. "Hi, Gina. Yes, she's right here."

"It's for you." He handed the phone to Sara and poured himself another cup of coffee, trying not to let on that he was listening to Sara's side of the conversation.

"Oh, Gina, that sounds nice, but I'm not sure how I could leave Gram."

She was quiet for a minute and then said, "Well, yes, Grandpa is here."

Jake had his back to Sara and grinned at Will and Gram.

"What is it, Darlin'?" Will asked Sara. "Does Gina need me for something?"

Sara asked Gina to hold on and turned to her grandfather and Gram. "She wants me to go to lunch with her today. I just don't think I should leave—"

"Now there is no reason you have to be chained to this house, Sara," Gram interjected. "Will can stay with me while you go have lunch."

"Well, then, with Grandpa here, I could take Meggie with me—"

"There's no need to take that baby. I can take care of her and Gram just fine," Will said.

"Or I could get one of the teens in to help this afternoon." Jake offered. "You need some time off for good behavior, Sara."

She held the receiver back to her ear. "Gina, I can make it. You'd think they all wanted to get rid of me today."

She smiled and nodded. "Yes, I know they are trying to take care of me. What time do you want to meet at the diner?"

Jake gave Will and Gram a thumbs-up sign and hoped the rest of his plan went half as well.

"Thank you all," she said when she got off the phone. "I do want to stop into the drugstore and pick up some pictures I took of Meggie anyway."

Satisfied that the first part of his plan was working, Jake kissed his daughter good-bye and headed out the door. But he turned back to Sara. "You have a good lunch, Sara, okay?"

Sara promised him she would and found herself looking

forward to lunch with Gina. By one o'clock, she'd fed Meggie her lunch and put her down for a nap. Gram and Grandpa should be able to handle things for a few hours, but she felt bad leaving them with no lunch fixed.

Grandpa shooed her out the door. "I'm perfectly capable of making us a grilled cheese sandwich or heating up leftovers in the fridge, Honey."

"I know, Grandpa."

"You just have a good time."

Gina was waiting at the diner when Sara got there. She'd made Deana promise to take a break and have lunch with the two of them when Sara showed up. Deana cooked most of the daily specials herself, but she did have two short order cooks and several waitresses, working two different shifts, to help out.

Deana brought their lunch to the table herself and turned to her help. "It's all yours. At least for an hour."

They just laughed at her.

"They know you too well, Deana," Sara said. "They know that all they have to do is give you that pitiful 'we need help' look, and you'll be on your feet and behind the counter in two seconds."

"Yeah, well, that's how it is when you own the place," Deana said.

"How is business these days, Deana? It always looks busier than ever when I'm in here." Gina took a bite of her roast beef sandwich.

"A little too good, some days. But I enjoy it." Deana grinned at her. "Oh, guess who was in here yesterday for early coffee?"

"David?" Gina asked.

Deana shook her head. "Nope."

"Luke and Jake?"

"Oh, they came in. But they aren't who I'm talking about."

Sara shrugged. "Okay, I give up. Who came in?"

"Nora. And she wasn't alone."

"Oh? Who was she with?"

"Dr. Wellington. And they were in very deep conversation until Nora seemed to get angry and flounced out of here."

Gina raised an eyebrow. "Well, so much for getting the two of them together."

Deana looked from one to the other. "You're wanting to play matchmaker?"

"Well, we'd thought they might make a good couple."

"They seemed to be getting along real well until Jake and Luke came in. Don't know what happened then. But the next thing I knew, Nora was hightailing it out of here."

"And what did Dr. Wellington do?" Gina asked.

"He chuckled and shook his head. Then he asked for another cup of coffee."

"I am going to have to meet this man," Sara said. "If Nora doesn't run him off, he may be just the man for her."

"I don't think he'd take any of her guff," Gina said.

"Exactly. I think she needs someone who isn't intimidated by her." Sara shrugged. "You know, someone who could let her bad moods roll right off of his back."

"That's a pretty tall order, Sara," Deana said. "I'm not sure that kind of man exists."

They all laughed and Sara sighed. "Well, we can hope."

The afternoon passed quickly. Deana wouldn't let either of them pay for lunch, and Gina wouldn't let her go back to Gram's.

"Ellie called me right after you left the house and said to tell you to make an afternoon of it. She called Maria and asked her to come over this afternoon."

"Maybe I've been crabby lately and they wanted a break from me."

Gina laughed. "You know better. They just don't want to wear you out."

At Sara's forlorn look, she relented and let her call to make sure Gram and Meggie were all right.

Once Sara heard Gram's voice and was assured all was well,

she was able to relax and enjoy the afternoon. She and Gina went window shopping and stopped to pick up the pictures she'd taken of Meggie earlier in the week, and of course they ended right back at the diner for afternoon coffee. They were poring over the pictures of Meggie when a shadow fell across the table. Two shadows. David and Jake stood next to them, grinning.

"Now why does it not surprise me to see the two of you here?" Gina asked.

"Probably because we planned to meet here this morning," David grinned and slid into the booth alongside his wife.

Jake smiled down at Sara and she slid over to make room for him. "And were you in on this plan, Jake?"

He chuckled and joined her in the booth. "You could say that. It took everyone to get you to take a break. You've been putting in some long hours lately. I just wanted you to know how much we—I—appreciate you."

"I. . .thank you, Jake." Taken aback by the compliment, Sara didn't quite know what to say. She slid the packet of snapshots over to him. "Here are those pictures of Meggie."

Jake grinned and pulled the packet closer. "Oh, Sara, these are wonderful. I haven't been the best at taking pictures of Meggie. Now I wish I'd taken more."

Sara pointed to one with Meggie asleep, her thumb stuck in her mouth and the teddy bear held tight in her arms. Another was of her playing with the puppy outside with Grandpa, and yet another had her sidling up to Gram and trying to share a cookie.

Jake looked at each picture and handed them to David. When he'd gone through them all, he looked into Sara's eyes. "Thank you."

"You're welcome. Would you like me to buy a photo album for them?"

"Let me look in Meggie's dresser. I'm pretty sure there's one there or in a box somewhere."

Sara nodded. "Okay. If you can't find one, I'll pick one up."

"Pssst, Sara," Gina whispered.

Sara looked over and saw Gina motioning to the other side of the diner.

"That's Dr. Wellington."

Sara turned her head and saw a tall, silver-haired man, about six feet tall and nicely built, sitting at a small table. He looked up at the waitress, and Sara could see that he had a wonderful smile.

She looked back at Gina. "He and Nora would look stunning together, wouldn't they?"

"What are you two up to now?" David asked.

"We aren't up to anything. Just hoping."

"About what?" Jake looked across the room. "Oh, he was in here with Nora yesterday, I think it was. She didn't stay long, though. She left right after Luke and I came in."

"We're hoping there might be a little romance in the air for them."

"Then you'd better pray about it," Jake said. "From what I saw, Nora wasn't too happy when she left here."

"But then it's hard to tell when Nora is happy, isn't it?" Gina asked.

"Sure is for me," Jake replied.

Gina looked over at the doctor and sighed. "Still, they would make a stunning couple."

"Wife of mine," David said, "you know it takes more than looking good together to make a good couple."

"Oh, yes, that I know," Gina grinned. "It takes love and trust and faith and God's blessing to make a good couple."

"And sometimes it takes years to get there," David added.

Gina leaned into the arm that surrounded her and nodded. "Sometimes it does."

Sara and Jake chuckled, knowing their friends were talking about themselves.

"And sometimes it takes knocking some chips off shoulders and rehashing old hurts to get to real healing." David winked at his wife.

"Sometimes it does." Gina repeated softly. They both shot Sara and Jake pointed looks.

"What?" Sara and Jake asked at the same time.

David slid out of the booth with Gina right behind him. He looked at Jake and Sara and smiled. "Dear friends, I think maybe it's time to bury that past of yours so you both can get on with the future. To that end, Gina and I are providing supper for Ellie, Will, and Meggie. Take your time."

With that, they walked out of the diner, leaving Jake and Sara at a loss for words.

Jake found his voice first. "I think my plans have just been sped forward." He shook his head and laughed out loud, bringing curious glances from nearby tables.

"Jake? What's so funny? And what plans are you talking about?" Sara asked.

He met her eyes and his laughter stopped. He reached out and twirled a piece of Sara's hair around his finger and smiled at her.

"I wanted to have a chance to talk to you without Meggie interrupting us, without you having to see to Gram and Will, without any of the hundred and one things you keep busy with at the house. So I came up with the plan to let you have an afternoon off."

"You had me spend the afternoon with Gina so you could talk to me? Jake, that doesn't make much sense." Sara pulled back and the tendril of hair slid through Jake's fingers.

"You needed an afternoon off. And it seemed the easiest way to get you to the diner. My plan was just to have coffee and then maybe stay awhile after Gina and David left. I didn't know they were going to add clearing up our past into the mix."

"Why didn't you just tell me you wanted to talk to me?"

"I was afraid you'd find something you just had to see to. It seems every time we're alone together for more than a couple of minutes, you find something that needs to be taken care of."

He was right. Sara was afraid that if they were alone for more than a few minutes, Jake might become aware of the love she felt for him and tried so hard to hide. She sighed lightly.

"Well, here we are," Sara said softly. "What do you want to talk about?"

He stared down at his coffee cup.

"Jake?"

He took a deep breath and looked into Sara's eyes. "I was wondering, if we could, well, if you would go to dinner with me one night."

"To dinner with you?" Sara looked confused.

Jake nodded. "You know, as in a dinner date?"

"A dinner date," she repeated. "With you?"

"Yes."

"Oh." Sara's heart seemed to do a double somersault before she could speak again. "I'd like that."

"You would?" Jake grinned. "I mean, you will?"

She nodded, feeling the color steal up her cheeks. What was wrong with her? She felt like a teenager being asked out for her very first date. "When?"

"How about Saturday night? Anywhere you want to go."

Sara smiled. Jake was as nervous as she was. "Anywhere is fine. You plan it."

Jake nodded. "All right. I'll pick you up at six-thirty if that's okay?"

"That'd be fine."

They were both silent for a minute.

"Jake?"

"Yeah?"

"I don't know if I'm supposed to go home now, or back to Gram's house to pick up Grandpa."

Jake smiled and shook his head. "Neither do I. I'm afraid my planning hadn't gotten much past asking you for a date."

Their eyes met and they burst into laughter, spontaneous, shared, and comfortable.

thirteen

Jake followed Sara back to his grandmother's house. True to their word, Gina and David were already there, and they asked Jake and Sara to join everyone for the pizza they'd had delivered.

Although Jake noticed several curious glances, no one asked why they'd returned early. And no one said a word when Jake asked Will if he was up to babysitting on Saturday night while he and Sara went out to eat.

Will just grinned and said, "You bet I am."

That was it. No teasing remarks or nosy questions. Just acceptance.

After everyone left and Jake put Meggie to bed, he remembered to look for the photo album he was sure he'd packed. Melissa had made it, and he'd like to at least get all of those first pictures of Meggie in the album her mother had created especially for her.

A quick look through Meggie's dresser drawers told him it wasn't there, so Jake took down the two boxes he'd put in the top of the closet when they'd first moved back. The first box held clothes Meggie had grown out of before they left Albuquerque, but the second one held the album. It was covered in baby print material, with a covered heart that a picture could be slipped inside of gracing the front.

Jake took the album downstairs to the kitchen where he'd left the photos of Meggie. He knew he hadn't put any pictures in the album, so he was surprised when he opened the album up and saw a photo of himself and Melissa on the very first page. He remembered when the photo had been taken—right before Meggie's birth. An envelope had been slipped in behind the photo.

Jake pulled it out and turned it over in his hands. It was addressed to him and Meggie in Melissa's handwriting and was dated only a month before she'd died. He opened the envelope and drew out a letter.

All the guilt he'd ever felt for not loving Melissa enough came to the surface as Jake unfolded the single page and read the very first line:

To my two loves, Jake and Meggie,

I pray you never have to read this, because it will mean I'm not with you. I've been told it's a normal thing to be afraid of childbirth, and I am. And no, Jake, there is nothing wrong that I know of. But just to put my mind at ease, I'm writing this in case something should happen to me during delivery and I don't have a chance to tell you both how very much I love you.

My dear sweet Meggie, how I looked forward to holding you in my arms and being the best mother I could be to you. But it's not to be, if this letter is being read, so I have to tell you and your daddy a truth.

Jake, my love, I'm sorry. For I did deceive you in the beginning. I was not pregnant when you married me. I took advantage of your honor because I wanted so much to be your wife. I'd loved you for so long, and yet I knew you didn't love me. You tried your best. I know that. And it's not your fault. I robbed you of your chance for happiness by grasping at my own. I'm sorry, Jake. I pray that you will forgive me and find that happiness with someone who will be a loving mother to our daughter.

Precious Meggie. Please listen and learn. Never try to trick someone into marrying you. Your daddy has been a wonderful husband and has tried to make me happy in every way possible. But the one thing I wanted, his love, is the one thing he couldn't completely give me. You see, it always belonged to another. Yet your daddy gave up the happiness he could have had for me. For what he thought was his responsibility. I lied to him to get him to marry me. And he stayed with me when there was no reason for him to do so, because of his beliefs and the faith that I took advantage of. So instead of one person being unhappy, there were three or more. I tell you this now, my sweet Meggie, so that you will be happy for your daddy when he finds his own happiness after all of these years. And to keep you from making the same mistakes I did.

I've asked God for His forgiveness, and I know that I have it. Now I ask your daddy to forgive me. He has promised to take you to church and teach you all the things I didn't learn until I was an adult. If we can show you how to always look to the Lord to lead your way, you'll be fine, my love. I could leave you in no better hands than those of the Lord above and your daddy. I love you both with all my heart,

Mommy Melissa

Jake pressed his eyes shut against the sudden sting of tears and took a deep steadying breath. Finally he knew the truth.

❧

Sara tried to stay busy to keep from getting nervous about her date with Jake. But it didn't work. And Nora didn't help matters. She called bright and early the next morning, and Sara could tell from the tone in her mother-in-law's voice that she wasn't at all happy.

"Sara, just what kind of hold does that man have over you?"

"Pardon me? What are you talking about, Nora?"

"I heard about you and Jake cozying up at the diner yesterday. I told you he only wants a mother for Meggie. Are you honestly going to let yourself be hurt by that man once more?"

"Nora—"

"I just can't stand by and let you do that without warning you, Sara. You are going to be hurt badly." With that, Nora hung up.

Sara stood looking at the receiver, shaking her head, at a total loss for words. She hung up the phone and sighed deeply. She truly didn't want to upset her mother-in-law, but the only way to avoid that would be to move to the ranch and never come into town, thereby avoiding running into Jake and Meggie at all. Sara knew that never had been an option.

Still, Nora's warning repeated itself over and over in her mind. Was Jake's only interest in her as a possible mother for Meggie? While she would love to have that role, she didn't want it without Jake's love.

She lost count of how many times that day she picked up the phone to cancel the date with Jake only to change her mind and hang up before the call went through. The truth was that she wanted to go out with him. She wanted to see where they were headed. Wanted to see if what she thought was happening between them really was. She hoped she wasn't in for more heartbreak.

Grandpa left for Gram's about thirty minutes before Jake was due to pick Sara up. Gina had called earlier to let Sara know that she and David were providing supper again for the two older people and Meggie, so she wouldn't have to worry about anything.

When Jake arrived a few minutes early, Sara was relieved that she didn't have time to get nervous. But when she opened the door to him, she knew she'd only been faking her serenity.

She'd decided to wear the aqua-and-yellow sundress she'd bought for his welcome-home party. As his glance took in what she was wearing and zeroed in on her mouth, she knew she'd worn it because it reminded her of the night when Jake had held her in his arms and kissed her. Noticing his eyes darken as he pulled his gaze away from her lips to her eyes, Sara was pretty sure he was also remembering that night.

"You—" Jake cleared his throat. "You look lovely."

"Thank you." He seemed almost as nervous as she felt, but he certainly looked handsome in dress slacks and a crisp white shirt, with his hair still damp from the shower. "You look very nice yourself."

She grabbed her purse and the wrap that came with the dress and locked the door behind her. They headed for Jake's car, and she savored the feel of his hand at the small of her back. He made her feel protected and special. "Where are we going?"

"Well, the choice is still yours, but I've been told there's a new restaurant just outside of town, Los Hacienda, that's very good. We could still go into Roswell or Ruidoso, if you'd rather."

"No. No, Los Hacienda sounds wonderful. I haven't been there yet, and I've heard the food is excellent."

"Well, I have to admit, I'm a little nervous about going too far away from Gram's right now."

Sara laughed as Jake opened the passenger door and she seated herself. "You must have read my mind. I kept thinking that we might want to be close by. Although Gina and David will be there, I'd still feel better if we don't go too far."

Jake smiled as he went around and took the driver's seat. Sara was already so protective of Meggie. Melissa couldn't have hand-picked a better mother for their child. But Jake knew Sara's mothering abilities had nothing to do with his asking her out. He wanted to be with Sara, the woman he'd come to love even more than the teenager he'd planned to marry.

Jake had been told to ask for a river table, and he'd done that when he'd made reservations the day before. Now he was impressed when they were led to the second floor and shown to a table set in its own little alcove, with a small balcony off to the side, overlooking the Hondo River below.

The waiter lit the candle on their table, filled their water glasses, told them of the day's specials, and left them with menus. He returned quickly with a basket of tortilla chips and salsa. They both decided on the special of the day and were left alone once more.

"Oh, Jake. This is really beautiful," Sara said, looking around at the warm interior and back out to the river.

"A fitting setting for a beautiful woman." Jake didn't take his eyes off her as she turned back to him. She was beautiful, her green eyes glowing, her auburn hair on fire in the candlelight. She took his breath away.

"Jake—"

"I mean it, Sara." Jake reached across the table and took her hand in his. "You are beautiful, inside and out. You always have been."

Jake could see the color rise in her face even in the dim candlelight. He felt the tremble of her fingers in his hand, but she didn't pull away. Feeling a hope he was almost afraid of, Jake reached over with his other hand and raised her chin so that her eyes met his. "I love you, Sara. I always have."

Sara's hand slid out of his and covered her heart. She shook her head and looked around as if she wanted to escape. She bolted from her chair and ran out to the private balcony.

Jake was right behind her. He turned her to face him. "Sara?"

"Jake, you don't mean what you are saying. You loved Melissa—"

"Sara, I know you didn't want to go into the past, but we have to. I was so wrong to lose my temper and leave so long ago. Can you ever truly forgive me?"

"You know that I already have forgiven you, Jake. There's no need for this—"

Jake's fingers gently touched her lips to quiet her. "Sara, please, hear me out. I need you to know that I understand I was the one who threw our relationship away. I was the one who didn't trust you, myself, or the Lord back then. And I ruined it all. I don't even remember the drive back to the university that night, but I know there was a party going on when I got there. I remember taking one beer, then two. I don't remember much after that. I got drunk, Sara. For the first and last time, yes, but I got royally drunk."

"Jake, we all make mistakes. You really don't have to do this."

Jake looked out over the vista before him, but saw nothing of its beauty. He rubbed the back of his neck and closed his eyes. He knew what he said next might end any chance he ever had with Sara, but he had to say it.

He opened his eyes and looked into hers. "By the time I came to my senses and realized I needed to apologize to you, it was too late."

"What do you mean, too late?" Sara asked.

"I know now that you didn't betray me that night. But I betrayed you. And that betrayal changed the course of my life." Jake reached into his pocket and pulled out the letter from Melissa.

"I didn't feel free to tell you this until I found this letter the other night." He handed it to Sara. "I'm not sure I'll ever give it to Meggie to read. Maybe the best thing to do is to leave it all behind. But I want you to read it, Sara. I want you to understand."

Sara unfolded the piece of paper Jake handed her, and he stood still, his heart pounding as he waited. When she looked back at him, her eyes were overflowing with tears.

"Oh, Jake." She handed the letter back to him and brushed at her wet cheeks. "I don't know what to say. I truly thought you'd broken up with me for Melissa. But I didn't know—"

Jake looked down into her shimmering eyes. "I'm so sorry, Sara. If I hadn't been so stubborn and jealous that night—"

"You wouldn't have Meggie now," Sara finished. "And neither of us would want that."

Jake never knew who reached out first, but suddenly, Sara was right where he wanted her to be—held tightly in his arms.

"I know you loved Wade and had a good life with him, Sara. I learned to love Melissa, and I will be eternally grateful to her for giving me my Meggie. But I've always felt we were meant to be together. I do love you, Sara. I know that I always will. Is there any way. . .do you think it is possible for us to start over and go on from here? Could there be a second chance for us?"

Sara released a sob and a joyful chuckle all at once. "Oh, Jake, I hope so. I truly hope so."

Jake crushed her in his embrace and claimed her lips. At her unhesitating response, he deepened the kiss with sweet promise. The past was buried and the future begun.

fourteen

Sara could never remember enjoying a meal more. She knew there were stars in her eyes and she didn't care who saw them. Jake loved her. Had always loved her. She was sure the joy she felt was obvious to anyone looking at her. It had to be.

If anyone asked her later what she'd eaten, she wasn't sure she would be able to tell them. All she knew for certain was that Jake loved her and she loved him. Nora had been wrong. Melissa's letter had put all her doubts to rest. Sara thanked the Lord for letting Jake find the letter and have her read it.

Jake paid the waiter and they were getting ready to leave when Sara turned to see Nora near the doorway, staring at them. Nora was with Dr. Wellington, but she pulled away from him and approached their table.

"I knew there was something going on between the two of you! I knew it!"

Dr. Wellington approached the table, looking apologetic, and put a hand through Nora's arm. "Nora, our table is ready. Please—"

Nora jerked her arm away. "Not until I've said what's needed to be said ever since Jake came back to town."

"Nora, please," Sara said. "You are creating a scene." She knew Nora would hate herself once she realized how she had behaved in public. Appearances meant everything to her.

"I don't care. I'm going to say this. Of all the people in the world for you to take up with, don't you know that Wade would turn over in his grave to know it was Jake? He worked so hard to win you. Even had me writing those anonymous notes to get Jake to doubt your love—"

"Nora!" Sara couldn't believe the woman's horrible rudeness or her awful admission.

Jake put his arm protectively around Sara.

"Nora, that's enough!" Dr. Wellington said. He pulled her to face him. "We are going to our table now. Or we are going home. Your choice."

Nora looked around as if she only now realized where she was and what she had done. Her hand grasped her chest, and she crumpled into a heap.

Sara knelt at the doctor's side as he checked Nora's vital signs. He picked her up.

"I'm taking her to the hospital right now. I don't want to wait for an ambulance."

Jake pulled Sara to her feet and gathered her purse and wrap. "We're right behind you."

❧

Hours later, Sara and Jake sat in the hospital waiting room, still uncertain of Nora's condition.

"Sara? Are you all right?" Jake asked. "Do you want me to get you some coffee, hot chocolate, anything?"

"No, Jake. Thank you, I'm fine. I just wish Dr. Wellington would let us know how she is. I knew she was stressed, I knew it. I should have spent more time with her."

"Sara, you can't blame yourself for this. Nora must have some kind of underlying problem. You are not to blame."

Sara sighed and lowered her head, rocking back and forth on the waiting room couch. "I don't want to take the blame, but I—"

"She's going to be fine, Sara." Dr. Wellington crossed the room and held out his hand. "I'm Michael Wellington. I wish we could be meeting under better circumstances."

"Nora? She's going to be all right? Did she have a heart attack? A stroke?"

The doctor shook his head. "No, she didn't. I am going to keep her in here at least overnight for observation, but it wasn't a heart attack or a stroke. She's put herself under a lot of stress in the last few years, but of course you know that."

Even though his arm encircled her, Jake felt Sara pulling

away from him inch by inch.

"Do you think she has a heart problem, Doctor?" he asked.

"No. At least not now, and none of the tests we've run show anything wrong with her heart. I do want her to undergo a stress test to be certain, but stress can cause a lot of problems when it's not under control, and it's obvious that the last year has taken its toll on Nora. I do apologize to you both for the scene she caused tonight."

Sara shook her head. "No, I should have seen this coming. I should have checked in on her more often. I should have seen that she was struggling."

"Sara. None of this is your fault. Nora brings a lot of this on herself."

Sara shook her head. "I should have known she needed me."

Jake exchanged glances with the doctor. He shrugged and shook his head.

"Well, right now Nora needs rest," the doctor said, "and I'll see that she gets it. You two should go on home. You can see her tomorrow."

Sara nodded and Jake shook Dr. Wellington's hand.

They walked out to Jake's car silently, but when he'd settled Sara and taken his seat, he turned to her before starting the car.

"Sara, Dr. Wellington is right. This isn't your fault."

Sara nodded. "I know. And it wasn't my fault that Wade and my baby were killed in the wreck. But if I hadn't wanted that ice cream, they might still be alive."

She looked over at Jake with tears in her eyes. When he reached to take her in his arms, she pulled back and shook her head. She sniffed and brushed at her tears.

"Jake, I'm not sure we can see each other again. I cannot take feeling responsible for something happening to Nora. I can't."

He wanted to yell and tell her she couldn't throw away what they had. Not now. But a quiet voice stopped him. *Trust in Me, always,* it said.

Jake listened and tried to stay calm. "Sara, I love you. I want to have a life with you."

Sara turned her face to the window. "I want that too, Jake. But right now I'm not sure it's going to be possible."

Jake took a deep breath. He'd waited this long, surely he could wait longer. And this time he was going to put his trust in the Lord.

ه

The next few days were some of the longest Sara had ever endured. Nora seemed to have slid into a deep depression, and she wasn't talking. At least not to Sara—even though Sara spent most of every day in Nora's room, reading to her, talking to her, anything to get her to respond.

Sara knew that Nora could talk if she wanted to. She'd heard her speaking to the nurses. But as soon as Sara walked into the room, she clammed up.

Dr. Wellington had ordered a battery of tests, but so far nothing unusual had shown up. Sara knew he cared for Nora, but at the same time he seemed frustrated with her.

Gram was getting around without the crutches now, and Lydia took over planning the family reunion, while Gina and the church family stepped in to help so that Sara could be with Nora.

But Sara missed being at Gram's. Her heart cried out for Meggie, and she was afraid the baby would feel she'd abandoned her. Her heart twisted each time she thought of what Jake must be feeling. He'd laid his soul bare for her, and she'd left him without an answer.

She'd never felt so torn in her life, Sara thought as she walked down the hospital corridor from Nora's room to the cafeteria. She and Jake had been on the verge of staking out a future for themselves and Meggie, but now, with Nora in the hospital and knowing how she felt about Jake, the future seemed bleaker than ever.

Sara wanted to be with Jake and Meggie, but how could she possibly start a new life when her mother-in-law refused to even talk to her about anything, much less her relationship with Jake?

Sara ran into Dr. Wellington in the cafeteria line, and he bought her lunch and himself a cup of coffee and asked if he could join her. Sara was glad to have a chance to talk to him. "Have any of the test results pointed to what is wrong with Nora, Dr. Wellington?"

"No. And they aren't going to tell us anything we don't already know. Nora is basically healthy. She's just let the stress in her life take over, instead of handing things over to the Lord."

"You're sure she didn't have a heart attack?"

"Yes, Sara, I'm sure. Her heart is healthy."

Sara tried to blink the tears of relief away. Dr. Wellington reached out and took her hand. "I know you care deeply for your mother-in-law. So do I. But we can't take on the blame for Nora's stress. She's gone through no more than you have in the last year, Sara. You can't let her health rule your life."

"But I don't want her to think she doesn't matter to me."

"Then tell her that she does and get on with your life. You have that right."

"I want Nora to be happy."

The doctor nodded. "So do I. And I'm going to do everything I can to see that she is. But in the end, Sara, I can't make her happy. You can't make her happy. She has to learn to let herself be happy."

"I know what you are saying is true. It's just so hard to walk away and start a new life, knowing I'm hurting her."

"And what she's done hasn't hurt you? And Jake?" He shook his head. "No wonder you're the one who has rings under her eyes. Look closely at Nora when you see her again."

"I think I know what you're telling me. I've been praying about it. I'm sure the Lord will let me know what to do."

Dr. Wellington looked at his watch and stood up. "I'm sure He will. I'm going to look in on Nora now. You relax and enjoy your lunch."

Sara tried to do just that. But mostly, she just prayed.

❧

Jake headed down the hall to Nora's room. He didn't know what else to do. If he waited for Sara to tell Nora to go fly a kite, he'd have a long wait. Yet all of this was taking its toll on her. He knew she loved him and Meggie. He could hear it in her voice when she called at night to see how Meggie and Gram were doing. He reassured Sara, but he didn't tell her that Meggie asked for her at least ten times a day. He couldn't put that kind of pressure on her. Neither could he ask her to marry him, knowing that Nora would never give them her blessing and would try to make Sara as unhappy as she could.

He'd just realized how very important family was to his daughter and to himself. And Nora was family. He had to try. But he dreaded the confrontation he knew was coming, and he stopped outside her room to gather his thoughts.

A male voice Jake recognized as Dr. Wellington's could be heard coming from the half-opened door. "Nora, you have got to get past this. You have to for Sara's sake, for your own sake. For our sake."

"I know I do, Michael," Nora cried. "It's just that Sara is all I have left of Wade, and she has been a daughter to me. But she loved Jake before she ever loved my son. I don't want to lose her, but I can't help but feel pushed aside. And I'm jealous. I wanted a grandchild so badly, and now Sara will get to be a mother, but I'm never going to be a grandmother."

Jake could hear sobbing from the other side of the door. His heart went out to his aunt, while at the same time he was appalled at her petty jealousy.

Judge not. Trust Me. The small voice made itself heard. Jake nodded. "I hear You, Lord," he whispered.

He needed the reminder. His jealousy had been the cause of his and Sara's first breakup. Now Nora's threatened to do the same. But this time, he was going to trust the Lord to lead his way. He bowed his head and said a quick prayer and then walked into Nora's room.

Nora's hand flew to her throat. "Jake! What—"

"Good afternoon, Jake," Dr. Wellington said, interrupting Nora, but he reached out and touched her shoulder. "It's good to see you again."

"Aunt Nora, Dr. Wellington." Jake strode into the center of the room. "I couldn't help but overhear part of your conversation."

His aunt's face paled as she looked at the doctor, who smiled at her and took her hand.

Jake cleared his throat. "I have a little girl who has a great-grandmother, and I'm hoping the woman I love will become her mommy. But every little girl needs a grammy."

The color began to return to Nora's face. "How about it, Aunt Nora? Want to make a deal?"

&

Sara finished her lunch, thinking over what Dr. Wellington had said. Nora didn't have heart trouble. She was going to be fine. All Sara could do for Nora was let her know she cared about her and would always be part of her family no matter who she married. If Nora would think rationally about it, she'd realize that marrying Jake would keep her in the family.

Sara disposed of her dirty dishes and headed back to Nora's room. She was going to take the doctor's advice and reassure her mother-in-law. Then she was going to Jake and Meggie and get on with her own life.

When she turned onto the corridor that led to Nora's room, Sara was surprised to see Jake outside the woman's room. He bowed his head before opening the door and entering. What was he doing? He knew how Nora felt about him. She hurried her pace until she arrived outside the room.

She entered quietly behind Jake, and what she heard sent a warm wave of love flooding through her heart. Jake was declaring his love for her and asking Nora to be a part of that love by being a grandmother to Meggie. He'd put his heart on the line with Sara, and now he was trying to make peace with Nora so that they could have a future.

Sara broke the silence that fell on the room. "Nora, if I were you, I'd take Jake up on his offer." She walked up to Jake and wrapped her arms around him. "I certainly plan to."

Jake's smile lit his face as he gathered Sara close. "Nora, I meant what I said. Meggie needs a grammy. Think about it."

Nora's mouth opened and shut, but for once, nothing came out. Dr. Wellington stood at her side, grinning.

Jake and Sara backed out of the room. "You can give us your answer later, Aunt Nora," Jake said. "Right now, we have a few things to settle." He pulled Sara into the hall and looked down into her eyes. "Did you mean it? Will you marry me and be a mommy for Meggie?"

"I will."

Jake picked her up and twirled her around right there in the hospital corridor. He bent his head and sealed her answer with a kiss that healed the past and promised a lifetime of love for the future.

epilogue

Dressed in lace, with her auburn hair swept up into an elegant french twist, Sara waited in the fellowship hall to begin her walk down the aisle behind her attendants, Deana and Gina. More nervous and happy than she could ever remember, she clung to her grandfather's arm, thinking back over the past few weeks since she and Jake had announced their engagement. Her heart filled with love for Jake, Meggie, their extended family, and friends, and she thanked the Lord for the blessings He'd bestowed on her.

There hadn't been any debate over the wedding date. As Gram stated, "What better time to have a wedding than on the Fourth of July? Everyone will be here for the family reunion, and by then your new home will be ready to move into."

Sara and Jake weren't about to argue. They'd waited such a long time to start their life together.

Nora had wasted no time in taking Jake up on his offer. She'd come to realize that the guilt she'd felt about sending Jake those anonymous notes all those years ago had surfaced when he'd moved back home. The fear and worry that he and Sara would discover what she had done had taken its toll on her health, but with the truth revealed and having received Jake and Sara's forgiveness, Nora began to count her blessings. By the end of that week, she was out of the hospital, helping Gram and Sara take care of Meggie while everyone in the family helped plan the wedding.

Sara let the school know that she wouldn't be teaching that fall. She and Jake had talked it over, and because Meggie had gone through so many changes in her young life, they decided that making sure she felt secure and loved was one of their top priorities. There would be plenty of time to teach once the toddler started school. Besides, Sara could think of nothing she'd rather do than enjoy the blessing God was giving her—to be Jake's wife and Meggie's mommy.

But the blessings hadn't stopped there. Nora was a different person. She'd turned into the woman Sara had only been given a glimpse of the night of Jake's welcome-home party. She was absolutely crazy about Meggie, and Meggie had taken to her as well. Nora would stay with Gram and help take care of Meggie while Jake and Sara went on a brief honeymoon to Santa Fe. And much to the delight of the whole family, Nora and Dr. Wellington had become an item around town.

Gram and Grandpa kept everyone guessing about their relationship. They seemed to be inseparable—chuckling and whispering together any time they were around each other—and Sara and Jake were sure they must be plotting and planning on how to add Dr. Wellington to the family.

"We're going to have to do something about those two," Sara had whispered to Jake the night before, as they'd watched their grandparents during the wedding rehearsal.

Jake nodded. "As soon as we get back from Santa Fe, we're going to have to do a little matchmaking ourselves."

Sara took a deep breath when she and Grandpa were given their signal and began their walk down the aisle. Her smile was tremulous, but she kept the tears of joy at bay by focusing on Jake.

With Luke and John by his side, Jake tried to hide his nervousness. But when Sara started down the aisle, he was sure his sigh of relief was audible. He couldn't take his eyes off her as she made her way to him, and he barely heard David ask who gave Sara away, or Will's answer. Finally she was standing by his side, and the moment he'd spent a lifetime waiting for had arrived.

Jake and Sara turned to David and exchanged their wedding vows in front of family, friends, and what must have been half the town. They were pronounced husband and wife, and Jake's lips claimed Sara's in a sweet promise to love her for the rest of their lives.

David introduced them as Mr. and Mrs. Jake Breland, and the two turned to face the loved ones who had just witnessed their promises to love, honor, and cherish each other. Jake smiled at his Meggie sitting contentedly in her Grammy Nora's lap, saw his grandmother and Sara's grandfather sitting side by side and Aunt Lydia and Uncle Ben behind them. The smiles of his and Sara's family and friends reflected their shared joy.

Jake pulled Sara's hand through his arm and looked down at his new bride before starting up the aisle. The love shining from her eyes had him swallowing the sudden lump in his throat, and he thanked the Lord for bringing him home, for bringing him and Sara together again, and for their ever-widening family circle.

Will nudged Ellie and whispered in her ear as they watched their grandchildren walk back up the aisle together. "Look at those two. We finally did it, didn't we, El? We finally got those two together."

"Oh, I think we had a lot of help from above, Will. We can't take all the credit ourselves," Ellie said softly, leaning closer to Will so that he could hear.

"That's true, El. Very true," Will nodded. "But, now that they are together and it looks like Nora has found a man who can handle her, maybe it's time we concentrated on ourselves for awhile. We aren't getting any younger, you know."

"I've been wondering when you were going to realize that, William Oliver. It's about time you made this courting you've been doing official," Ellie said, patting Will's cheek.

He quickly captured her hand and brought it to his lips. "Consider it done, my sweet Ellie. Consider it done."

The wedding party spilled out onto the church grounds just as the first fireworks from the Independence Day celebration began crackling in the night sky. Jake pulled Sara close to his side, and as he bent his head to kiss her once more, the fireworks surrounding them reflected the pure light of love bursting forth from their hearts.

A Letter To Our Readers

Dear Reader:

In order that we might better contribute to your reading enjoyment, we would appreciate your taking a few minutes to respond to the following questions. We welcome your comments and read each form and letter we receive. When completed, please return to the following:

Rebecca Germany, Fiction Editor
Heartsong Presents
PO Box 719
Uhrichsville, Ohio 44683

1. Did you enjoy reading *Family Circle* by Janet Lee Barton?
   ☐ Very much! I would like to see more books
      by this author!
   ☐ Moderately. I would have enjoyed it more if

   _____

   _____

   _____

2. Are you a member of **Heartsong Presents**? Yes ☐ No ☐
   If no, where did you purchase this book?_____

   _____

3. How would you rate, on a scale from 1 (poor) to 5 (superior), the cover design?_____

4. On a scale from 1 (poor) to 10 (superior), please rate the following elements.

   _____ Heroine   _____ Plot

   _____ Hero   _____ Inspirational theme

   _____ Setting   _____ Secondary characters

5. These characters were special because _____

   _____

   _____

6. How has this book inspired your life? _____

   _____

   _____

7. What settings would you like to see covered in future
   Heartsong Presents books? _____

   _____

   _____

8. What are some inspirational themes you would like to see
   treated in future books? _____

   _____

   _____

9. Would you be interested in reading other **Heartsong
   Presents** titles?   Yes ❏   No ❏

10. Please check your age range:
    ❏ Under 18   ❏ 18-24   ❏ 25-34
    ❏ 35-45   ❏ 46-55   ❏ Over 55

Name _____

Occupation _____

Address _____

City _____ State _____ Zip _____

Email _____

CAROLINA

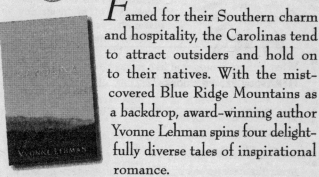

*F*amed for their Southern charm and hospitality, the Carolinas tend to attract outsiders and hold on to their natives. With the mist-covered Blue Ridge Mountains as a backdrop, award-winning author Yvonne Lehman spins four delight-fully diverse tales of inspirational romance.

Here's your ticket for a refreshing escape to the mountains. Enjoy the view as God works out His will in the lives of those who put their trust in Him.

paperback, 464 pages, 5 ³/₁₆" x 8"

❤ ❤ ❤ ❤ ❤ ❤ ❤ ❤ ❤ ❤ ❤ ❤ ❤ ❤ ❤ ❤ ❤

Please send me _____ copies of *Carolina*. I am enclosing $5.97 for each.
(Please add $2.00 to cover postage and handling per order. OH add 6% tax.)

Send check or money order, no cash or C.O.D.s please.

Name_____

Address _____

City, State, Zip _____

To place a credit card order, call 1-800-847-8270.
Send to: Heartsong Presents Reader Service, PO Box 721, Uhrichsville, OH 44683

❤ ❤ ❤ ❤ ❤ ❤ ❤ ❤ ❤ ❤ ❤ ❤ ❤ ❤ ❤ ❤ ❤

····Hearts♥ng ·····

HEARTSONG PRESENTS *TITLES AVAILABLE NOW:*

(If ordering from this page, please remember to include it with the order form.)

······Presents······

_HP341 IT ONLY TAKES A SPARK, *P. K. Tracy*
_HP342 THE HAVEN OF REST, *A. Boeshaar*
_HP345 THE PLAN, *L. Lyle*
_HP346 DOUBLE TAKE, *T. Fowler*
_HP349 WILD TIGER WIND, *G. Buck*
_HP350 RACE FOR THE ROSES, *L. Snelling*
_HP353 ICE CASTLE, *J. Livingston*
_HP354 FINDING COURTNEY, *B. L. Etchison*
_HP357 WHITER THAN SNOW, *Y. Lehman*
_HP358 AT ARM'S LENGTH, *G. Sattler*
_HP361 THE NAME GAME, *M. G. Chapman*
_HP362 STACY'S WEDDING, *A. Ford*
_HP365 STILL WATERS, *G. Fields*
_HP366 TO GALILEE WITH LOVE, *E. M. Berger*
_HP369 A TOUCHING PERFORMANCE, *G. O'Neil*
_HP370 TWIN VICTORIES, *C. M. Hake*
_HP373 CATCH OF A LIFETIME, *Y. Lehman*
_HP374 THE LAST COTILLION, *D. Mills*
_HP377 COME HOME TO MY HEART, *J. A. Grote*
_HP378 THE LANDLORD TAKES A BRIDE, *K. Billerbeck*
_HP381 SOUTHERN SYMPATHIES, *A. Boeshaar*
_HP382 THE BRIDE WORE BOOTS, *J. Livingston*
_HP385 ON THE ROAD AGAIN, *G Sattler*

_HP386 DANCE FROM THE HEART, *L. T. Jones*
_HP389 FAMILIAR STRANGERS, *G. Fields*
_HP390 LOVE ABOUNDS, *A. Bell*
_HP393 BEYOND PERFECT, *J. Peterson*
_HP394 EQUESTRIAN CHARM, *D. Mills*
_HP397 MY NAME IS MIKE, *G. Sattler*
_HP398 THE MUSHROOM FARMER'S WIFE, *U. McManus*
_HP401 CASTLE IN THE CLOUDS, *A. Boeshaar*
_HP402 SECRET BALLOT, *Y. Lehman*
_HP405 THE WIFE DEGREE, *A. Ford*
_HP406 ALMOST TWINS, *G. Sattler*
_HP409 A LIVING SOUL, *H. Alexander*
_HP410 THE COLOR OF LOVE, *D. Mills*
_HP413 REMNANAT OF VICTORY, *J. Odell*
_HP414 THE SEA BECKONS, *B. L. Etchison*
_HP417 FROM RUSSIA WITH LOVE, *C. Coble*
_HP418 YESTERYEAR, *G. Brandt*
_HP421 LOOKING FOR A MIRACLE, *W. E. Brunstetter*
_HP422 CONDO MANIA, *M. G. Chapman*
_HP425 MUSTERING COURAGE, *L. A. Coleman*
_HP426 TO THE EXTREME, *T. Davis*
_HP429 LOVE AHOY, *C. Coble*
_HP430 GOOD THINGS COME, *J. A. Ryan*
_HP433 A FEW FLOWERS, *G. Sattler*
_HP434 FAMILY CIRCLE, *J. L. Barton*

Great Inspirational Romance at a Great Price!

Heartsong Presents
Love Stories Are Rated G!

That's for godly, gratifying, and of course, great! If you love a thrilling love story but don't appreciate the sordidness of some popular paperback romances, **Heartsong Presents** is for you. In fact, **Heartsong Presents** is the *only inspirational romance book club* featuring love stories where Christian faith is the primary ingredient in a marriage relationship.

Sign up today to receive your first set of four never before published Christian romances. Send no money now; you will receive a bill with the first shipment. You may cancel at any time without obligation, and if you aren't completely satisfied with any selection, you may return the books for an immediate refund!

Imagine. . .four new romances every four weeks—two historical, two contemporary—with men and women like you who long to meet the one God has chosen as the love of their lives. . . all for the low price of $9.97 postpaid.

To join, simply complete the coupon below and mail to the address provided. **Heartsong Presents** romances are rated G for another reason: They'll arrive *Godspeed!*